WILLIAM L. COLEMAN

Chesapeake Charlie
and the
HAUNTED
SHIP

BETHANY HOUSE PUBLISHERS
MINNEAPOLIS, MINNESOTA 55438
A Division of Bethany Fellowship, Inc.

Chesapeake Charlie and the Haunted Ship
William L. Coleman

Library of Congress Catalog Card Number 82-73912
ISBN 0-87123-282-0

Published by Bethany House Publishers
A Division of Bethany Fellowship, Inc.
6820 Auto Club Road, Minneapolis, Minnesota 55438

Printed in the United States of America

Dedicated to
John and Michael Coleman

Special Thanks

Jim Coleman did extensive work collecting material and proofreading the manuscript for this book. His help is greatly appreciated.

Cindy Jensen did an excellent job of typing the manuscript.

About the Author

WILLIAM L. COLEMAN is a graduate of the Washington Bible College in Washington, D.C., and Grace Theological Seminary in Winona Lake, Indiana. He has pastored three churches: a Baptist Church in Michigan, a Mennonite Church in Kansas, and an Evangelical Free Church in Aurora, Nebraska. He is a Staley Foundation Lecturer. The author of some seventy-five magazine articles, his by-line has appeared in *Christianity Today, Eternity, Campus Life,* and several other Christian magazines. Coleman is best known for his devotional books for children. He is the father of three and makes his home in Nebraska.

Other books in this series

Chesapeake Charlie and the Bay Bank Robbers
Chesapeake Charlie and Blackbeard's Treasure
Chesapeake Charlie and the Stolen Diamond

Chapter One

"Why do you want to play this dumb game?" Laura huffed at Charlie.

"They always catch us," Kerry grumbled. "Every morning we get here early. We tease those guys on the playground and they chase us."

"Sure," Laura said, "and they always catch us. They *always* catch us. Now that's dumb."

"Not this time," Charlie replied. The trio walked briskly toward the school door. Charlie carried a brown sack under his left arm and stared stubbornly ahead.

"Sooner or later, Chesapeake Charlie figures out a solution," he bragged. "You can count on that."

"A few minutes later they found themselves on the second floor of the school, looking down a short hallway. At the end of the hall were three large, cardboard barrels. School supplies were stacked haphazardly on the barrel tops.

"All we have to do is get them this far," Charlie explained. "After that, we're the winners."

"What if the teachers catch us up here?" Kerry objected.

"No chance. No one uses these rooms until second period."

"Big deal," Laura said with a groan. "So they chase us here and then catch us. What does that prove?"

"That's where the mastermind comes in. Take a couple of these jars of petroleum jelly—and we'll have to hurry."

Charlie handed them the containers and some dirty rags.

"You've finally flipped," Laura said. "I knew your fan belt was loose, but this time it's snapped."

"My mother isn't going to like this," Kerry whimpered.

"Cut the belly-aching. We have to hurry if this is going to work."

Twenty minutes later the schoolyard was packed with students milling around. Some played soccer while others threw a football back and forth. The continuous talking created a loud, steady hum broken only by an occasional shout.

"Hey, spaghetti legs!" Charlie yelled at a tall boy dressed in jeans and a red jacket. "Yeah, you! Did anybody ever tell you that you run like a rubber duck?"

"Oh, yeah? We didn't have any trouble catching you yesterday!" The boy's two friends stood up stiffly as if they were about to lurch forward.

"That was my slow day," Charlie taunted. "You guys run like dump trucks."

"Get 'em!" the tall boy shouted, and two groups of three kids dashed toward the building.

Laura led the pack with her ponytail bobbing behind. Kerry took short, choppy steps and looked directly ahead, hoping to reach the school door. Arms flying loosely, Charlie whooped like an Indian as he raced across the yard. His wide grin and sparkling eyes showed how much he loved it.

The first three hit the door in a tight cluster and

scrambled upstairs. The pursuers were barely twenty feet behind and never lost sight of their victims.

When Charlie, Laura and Kerry reached the hallway they swung to the right and vanished into an empty classroom. Unable to see them, the chasers burst straight down the hall. The boy in the red jacket was the first to lose his footing on the slick floor. He fell like a shot duck and slid down the short hall in a sitting position. He smacked the barrels like a bowling ball. Art supplies shot into the air and purple paint splattered across his face.

The second boy was unable to apply his brakes and landed on his stomach. Head first, his body greased across the floor and into the barrels. Glue and paste tumbled onto the helpless boys.

The third fought it for a couple of seconds but was unable to hold his balance. Finally he collapsed and joined his friends in a perfect baseball slide.

Charlie, Laura and Kerry roared as they watched through the glass in the classroom door. Tears were rolling down their red faces as they doubled over with laughter.

"What's going on up here?" a shout came from the hall.

"Oh, no!" Kerry gasped.

"It's Mr. Taylor," Laura choked.

"You boys can't run inside the b— Ohhh!" The teacher's feet began to fly and his arms swung in every direction.

When Mr. Taylor hit the floor Charlie squinted his eyes as if he could feel the teacher's pain. The man's arms and legs sprawled in every direction. Mr. Taylor sailed toward the barrels. As he collided into the three boys, one last jar of orange paint tottered and then tumbled over the side. The bright goo ran down the left side of the teacher's head and onto his suit jacket.

"Charlie, why do you get carried away?" Mr. Dean asked sternly. "I'm not going to ground you any longer, but I don't want any more complaints from school. You aren't usually like this. I'd better not hear from the school again."

"You won't, Dad. I promise."

It felt good to be free. Two weeks was a long time to be grounded, especially when there were so many things to do around Collins Landing. He loved the Bay as it lapped up against the shore of his backyard. It held mystery, adventure, enjoyment and intrigue. All around the Bay there were living creatures waiting to be seen and understood.

Charlie sat on the picnic bench in his yard and ruffled the back of Throckmorton's neck. He thought again of how happy he was to live here, and how marvelous it was to watch the sea gulls arch against the sky, feel the dampness in the air and smell the brackish water. Throckmorton became drowsy as his back was rubbed; he was not an ambitious beagle.

A voice cracked the silence. "So your father finally let you loose."

Charlie stood but didn't bother to turn.

"If you ask me, he should have grounded you until you were a hundred and seven." Laura kept walking toward the bench. "I told my parents it was all your idea—and they didn't have any trouble believing me."

"Don't talk so much," Charlie's hand motioned for Laura to calm down. "Look, the bombers are flying." His arm thrust up to point toward the soaring sea gulls.

Not far down the shoreline they could see a white bird lift itself above a pile of rocks. The sea gull held steady, then dropped a hard object from its mouth.

"He's breaking clams." Charlie's wide smile looked like he had never seen it before. The common sights of the Bay still amazed this curious adventurer. He could barely hear the clam shatter against the rocks.

"They must be smart birds. How else could they figure out how to do that?"

"What? Drop clams on a rock? How big a brain would that take?"

"Why is it that girls never understand? How else would they open clam shells and eat dinner?"

"Anything you say, Charlie Dean. Why don't you open a sea gull circus? People could pay five dollars to see a bird drop clams on a rock.—'Step right up, ladies and gents. . .' "

Charlie turned and glared at Laura. His face twisted in agony. *Girls are hopeless*, he thought.

"I'm going to get my binoculars." Charlie started toward his back door.

"Wait a minute," Laura said. "I've got something important to discuss."

"Not if you're going to make fun of the sea gulls."

"Never mind—I'm sure they're brilliant. We'll send one to medical school."

"That does it, I'm leaving."

"You sure are touchy. You've been in the house too long. Stand still and I'll tell you why I came over."

"Say it quick."

"My uncle Gary invited me to go oystering tomorrow morning. He's going to dive for oysters and he said I could bring a friend."

"And you are asking *me*, a boy?"

"Well, you're nearly human."

"I hate to have to go with a girl. But I would like to see them dive. Hey, I thought it was bad luck to take a girl on an oystering boat."

"Uncle Gary doesn't buy that superstition stuff."

"Maybe this time. I'll have to check with my parents, but it sounds all right."

"Be at my place at 5:00 A.M. Bring a lunch."

Anything new got Charlie's curiosity up. Anything different set his mental wheels spinning. And naturally, anything about the Bay had to be explored immediately. Charlie would read about oystering before tomorrow.

Fall in the Chesapeake area can be terribly cool just before dawn, but that didn't bother Charlie and Laura. The excitement of going out on the water kept them both warm.

Gary looked too young to be Laura's uncle but he had been catching oysters for years. His boat, the *Retriever*, was old, but neat as a computer—everything in its place and a paint job that almost sparkled in the early sunlight.

"This is my partner, Mike," Gary announced to Charlie and Laura. "He'll haul up the oysters while I dive."

The *Retriever* was soon cutting across the Bay in search of deep water. As the darkness continued to lift, they saw several boats hunting for good oystering spots.

"We'll stop here—it's about 30 feet," Gary said as he cut the engine. "There ought to be some large oysters here."

"The tongers and dredgers can't get into the deep

crevices," Mike continued. "If we don't get those oysters, no one will."

"You want to throw that bottle over?" Gary asked Charlie.

Eagerly he tossed the plastic milk bottle buoy over the side. Mike then threw a red and white diver's flag over to warn other boats that someone was working under the water.

Gary squeezed into his rubber suit, tightened his weightbelt and adjusted his mouthpiece. This would allow him to handpick oysters for a couple of hours. When he filled a basket, Gary would tug on the rope and Mike would haul up the oysters.

In a few minutes Gary slid over the side and disappeared into the dark water. Charlie and Laura peered into the water, anxious to get a glimpse of the diver. They couldn't see Gary, but it was easy to follow his air bubbles as they surfaced.

Twenty minutes later Mike lifted a wire basket from the water. Charlie hurried to his side and helped carry the almost-eighty pounds of oysters and dumped them into a culling tray. Busily Laura joined in as they sorted through the dripping pile.

Only two or three shells were thrown back, plus one oyster that was too small to keep. It seemed much easier than the tonging Charlie had done a few times before.

With a little time to spare, Laura took off her gloves and held a warm cup of hot chocolate. The air was just cold enough to be uncomfortable.

"Your dad ever tell you much about the oyster wars?" Charlie asked Laura as he edged closer.

"Not much," she replied, sipping her drink.

"It must have been terribly dangerous." He inched

closer. "Some weeks they would find five or six bodies floating in the Bay."

"Who killed them?"

"Some were shot by other oystermen. Others got picked off by the Oyster Navy. Plenty of lead flying in every direction."

Smoothly Charlie slipped something into Laura's empty glove.

"Not only that," he continued, "but some people were kidnapped and forced to work on the boats. Their bodies were later found in the Bay."

"You make it sound like an awful place."

"No," Charlie protested. "The Bay has always been a great place, but it can be a dangerous place, too. It was just that some people thought there should be laws about oystering, and others thought it was a free country and that the watermen should do whatever they wanted."

"And they shot people because of those slimy oysters?"

"Oysters meant big money. They were being shipped all over the world from the Bay. The watermen who used tongs didn't get along with those who dredged with machines. The tongers thought the Bay was being ruined, so they shot at the dredgers."

"Couldn't the police stop it?"

"Not once it got going. They set a limit on how many oysters could be dredged but that seemed to make it worse. Before long, the tongers were shooting at the dredgers, the dredgers were shooting back and the police were shooting at everybody. That's why the state organized the Oyster Navy."

"How did the wars end?"

"Too many people were getting killed. The state

police backed off and soon everyone stopped fighting. It's been pretty quiet now for almost 30 years."

"Got a heavy one," Mike called out as he pulled another basket aboard.

Charlie darted to his side and Laura grabbed her gloves. Chuckling quietly, Charlie helped lift the bulky container.

"Ahhhhhhh!" Laura's scream could have cracked a rock. She threw her glove to the deck and screamed again. Mike and Charlie turned toward the shaken girl. Mike wondered what creature had attacked her while Charlie folded over in uncontrollable laughter.

"It's in the glove!" she yelled.

Hurriedly Mike grabbed the glove and shook it upside down. Finally something dropped to the deck—a slimy, cold, shapeless, gray, shell-less oyster.

"Ohhh," Laura said with a shiver. "You creep." Laura oozed out each word painfully. "You lowlife, Charlie Dean. You heartless snail."

The rest of the morning Charlie walked wide circles around the seething Laura. Never quite sure how she might strike, he kept a nervous eye alert at all times.

Gary came up for the third time just before noon, to eat and rest.

"How heavy are those weights?" Charlie asked as Gary unbuckled them.

"Fifty-five pounds. But that's the easy part. The air tanks check in at around a hundred thirty. Out of the water, it's like lugging a truck around."

"How many divers are looking for oysters in the Bay?" Laura wondered.

"I hear a couple hundred now," Gary added. "Some say it will save the oyster industry, others say it will ruin it. That's the way it always is with something new."

"It sounds like a great life to me," Charlie concluded. "Maybe I'll dive for oysters—after I get my Ph.D., of course."

"Some people think the oyster industry will be gone from the Bay in fifteen to twenty years," Gary explained. "I don't think so or I'd do something else. If we use our heads, there will be plenty of oysters a hundred years from now."

The afternoon went well with the crew on deck keeping fairly busy. By four o'clock, Charlie counted forty-two bushels stacked neatly and ready for the cannery. It had been a long day and Laura could feel the tautness in her face.

Finally Gary gave up and climbed back into the craft. Mike turned on the engine and aimed for shore.

"A real good day," Gary said after he changed clothes. "I can't see much down there, but it gives me a chance to feel how big the oysters are. If they aren't legal size I leave them. I can get them next year."

"You mind if I ask how much you get for a bushel?" Laura quizzed as she took a soft step behind Charlie.

"If I'm lucky I'll get nine dollars a bushel. It can differ from day to day."

"That sounds pretty good," she said as her left hand reached for the back of Charlie's belt. With smooth precision Laura grabbed his black belt and pulled it back. Quickly her right hand dumped a soggy oyster down Charlie's trousers.

"Ohhh!" Charlie felt it immediately. He danced frantically, stepping higher than any war whooper known to man.

"You louse!" he yelled, increasing his pace. "Get it out!" he shouted as he pulled at his pant leg.

Laura, Mike and Gary were holding their sides too tightly to be of any help. The greater Charlie's gyrations, the louder the three of them roared.

After several desperate seconds, the motionless oyster was shaken out of the bottom of Charlie's trousers. Exhausted, he plummeted onto the wooden bench.

"This isn't funny," Charlie insisted as he breathed heavily. "I like a joke as much as anybody, but this is too far. That cold slime could have frozen to my leg. I might catch pneumonia."

Not only did they not answer Charlie, they were laughing so hard, they probably never heard him.

The evening sun was slipping into the horizon as the *Retriever* neared the shore. In the chilly evening the shallow water reflected colors like a well-made mirror.

"Nearly every night I see that old freighter," Gary told Charlie and Laura, pointing to an old ship silhouetted against the sky.

"It's been sitting there for years and no one has bothered to claim it. It's rusted out, but there still must be some money in it as scrap metal."

"It must be wedged in the rocks," Laura suggested.

"Isn't there a name on it?" Charlie asked.

"Can't tell," Gary said. "Besides, I hear there's an old man living on it—kind of like a hermit. I've never seen him. A guy'd have to be half crazy to live on that."

That's curious, thought Charlie, *very curious.*

Chapter Two

"I don't really know much about it," Mr. Dean said as he backed the car out of the driveway. "It's been sitting at Yater Point for four or five years, I suppose."

Charlie leaned forward. "Is it a freighter?"

"I think so—a small one," Mr. Dean answered.

"It's a shame to let it rust away like that," Mrs. Dean joined in. "Doesn't help the beauty of the Bay."

"They say an old man lives on it"—Charlie's brother, Pete, had sat quietly until now—"a crazy coot."

Each member of the Dean family was dressed neatly. Neither of the boys cared to wear a tie to church, but Mr. Dean wore one practically every Sunday.

"I hope you two aren't thinking about trying anything too adventurous," Mr. Dean said as he drove the car through town. "The old freighter is no place for children. There may be rotten floors, huge rats—and there is no telling what else."

"Besides," Mrs. Dean turned to face the boys, "that story about the hermit. . . ."

"What's a hermit?" Pete asked.

"A man who lives alone and usually has some strange habits," Mrs. Dean explained. "I want you boys to stay away from that ship. There is plenty to do without doing something foolish."

"Do both of you understand that?" Mr. Dean twisted to look at his sons in the backseat. "Neither one of you has permission to go on that old ship."

Charlie and Pete each stared out a window and avoided their father's eyes. Their minds were busy with thoughts of exploring, mystery and excitement.

They soon arrived at a white frame church, similar to many others on the Eastern Shore. Stained glass windows provided bright colors around the building and a wooden steeple made it appear tall, strong and dependable.

The Dean boys did not often say so, but they enjoyed Pastor Crocket. He told many stories, had a good sense of humor and everyone knew he cared for people. They didn't often go to him with problems, but they knew they could if they wanted to.

Charlie wished there were cushions for the hard, straight-backed pews. On some Sundays, he was sure his fingertips, nose and jaw ached from sitting still so long.

The wood floor was slanted forward to help everyone see over the heads in front, but when Mr. Harrison sat in front of Charlie, the normal hour seemed like three days. The edges of Mr. Harrison's balding head would twitch for no apparent reason. Each twitch sent Charlie into uncontrollable giggling. He felt it wasn't his own fault, but his laughter angered his parents. He tried his hardest to remain quiet. Charlie dreaded it when Mr. Harrison sat in his section of the church; muffled giggles, pain and trouble usually followed.

Charlie believed children had a special gift when it came to church. They could half-listen to a sermon and do something else at the same time. Parents couldn't do that. They had to stare straight at the minister.

Pete pulled a blue crab claw out of his pocket and passed it to his brother. Charlie could hear Reverend Crocket talking about Lazarus. He didn't get *every* word, but that didn't seem important.

Pete showed Charlie an old scout knife. That seemed more interesting, but Pete wouldn't let him hold it.

By now Reverend Crocket had Lazarus raised from the dead and the religious leaders in an uproar.

Digging deeper into his pocket, Pete drew out a plastic bag of assorted marbles—large, blue blockbusters, small green soldiers, and more.

"You owe me a bag," Charlie whispered, grabbing the sack.

"Back off."

"Let me see."

"Cool it."

"Shhh."

"Let go."

R-r-r-r-i-i-p!

Clunk! Clunk! Clunk! Clunk! Clunk!

Heads turned briskly toward the two boys. The marbles bounced on the hardwood floor and began to roll toward the platform, the pulpit and Rev. Crocket.

Clunk! Clunk! Clunk! Clunk!

Charlie was afraid they would bounce forever. To him and Pete, each one sounded like a crisp cannon shot.

Rev. Crocket had stopped preaching and was staring in amazement at the two boys. Elderly members stretched their necks and peered through bifocals.

Charlie tried to smile back, but could barely produce a sober grin. *If only Mr. Harrison had sat in front of me,* Charlie thought. *If I'd been watching his head twitch, I wouldn't have been fighting over those dumb marbles.*

"It's not that big a deal," Charlie argued. "One."

"But what about the old man?" Laura asked.

"No one knows if there is an old man. Two, it's just a rumor. No one has actually seen him. Three."

Each push-up stretched the veins in Charlie's arms. The grassy backyard was the best gymnasium he could imagine. Throckmorton chased an occasional bird, but never got very close.

"I enjoy exploring as much as anyone, Charlie, but I don't want to run into the hairy arms of some weirdo inside an old boat." Laura threw a stick and Throckmorton pounced after it.

"I understand if you are afraid. Five. Girls are just that way. Six."

"Don't 'girls are just that way' me. I can hold my own with any creepy guy." Laura tossed the stick again. "Besides, your parents told you not to go near the ship."

"Seven. My parents still furnish guidance for me, but they realize I'm old enough to make decisions. Eight."

"That's a big lie. Your parents told you not to do it." Laura stood and began to walk away.

"Think it over. Ten. If you get up enough nerve, you might want to join the expedition. Eleven. If not, I suppose we'd better just take along some brave young *man.* Twelve."

"Charlie Dean, sometimes you make me so mad." Laura had walked further away. "Oh, what's the use of talking to you?"

Laura threw the stick high. It arched and landed

flat on Charlie's bobbing back. Instantly, Throckmorton ran across the yard and leaped toward the stick. With all his weight, the beagle collapsed on Charlie's back and both of them tumbled to the ground.

"Get off! Get off, you water buffalo."

Looking confused, Throckmorton remained perched on Charlie, while Laura, holding her sides in laughter, ran out of the yard.

"Girls!" Charlie grunted.

Throckmorton licked Charlie's face.

"Don't look so suspicious," Kerry warned in a loud whisper. All four were afraid of raising their voices.

"All we're doing is crabbing." Laura wiggled the string she held.

"Stay down, Throckmorton." Pete pushed on the beagle's head.

"Paddle a little closer to the ship," Charlie ordered Kerry. "There must be some way to board this old crate."

"Not so fast," Laura cautioned. "We haven't decided whether or not to climb on. You said we were 'just looking.'"

"Just looking is right. We haven't made up our minds yet." Charlie surveyed the rusted hull.

"I'm not sure I want to get on that ship this late, anyway." Kerry kept rowing. "It's almost dark."

"Row around to the port side," Charlie directed.

"Port side?" Kerry puzzled.

"Yes, that's the *left* side to you land lubbers."

As they pulled closer a loud creak came from the ship. Pete hugged Throckmorton and Laura dropped her string.

"Look," Charlie said as he pointed, "that must be a ladder. Let's row closer."

"What do you mean 'Let's row closer'? " Kerry snarled. "I don't see any 'let's' rowing. I'm the only one holding the oars."

"Shhh."

At the middle of the short, almost stubby ship, hung a rusty metal ladder. Some of its bolts were missing and it dangled loosely.

"That thing will never hold us." Pete rubbed the beagle's neck.

"No one said we were going to use it." Laura's voice was unsteady.

"Hermits can really be strange," Kerry cautioned. "They don't like anybody. That's why they live alone."

"Will you guys dry your tears? In the first place we don't know that anyone lives on this." Charlie reached up to grab the bottom rung of the ladder. "I say it's time to find out what's up here. You grandmas stay in the boat if you want to."

Charlie pulled himself up and wiggled a foot on the step.

Laura stood up. "Charlie, you're crazy!"

"It won't take me long." Charlie moved quietly to the top of the ladder.

"I can't let you go alone." Laura grabbed the ladder. "You could get yourself hurt."

Kerry pulled in the oars and followed. "My mother isn't going to like this."

"Throckmorton, you guard the boat." Pete lashed the boat to the ladder and started climbing.

"Shhh!" Laura tried to keep everyone quiet as they dropped from the rail onto the deck.

"Stay close—I'll lead the way," Charlie commanded. "If there's trouble we'll need each other."

The sun kept sliding slowly out of the sky, trying to

end the day. Cool evening air was settling in for the night. As the small herd of intruders tiptoed across the deck they kept looking in all directions. They found it difficult to stay calm when their stomachs were quivering like guitar strings.

They reached a doorway and looked down a dark stairway.

"I can barely see anything," Kerry complained.

"There's enough light." Charlie swallowed hard and started down into the cave-like darkness.

Bang, Bang.

Charlie jumped back up the steps and lunged out onto the deck.

"What was that?" asked Laura.

"It was just me," answered Pete. "I kicked a gas can."

"Thanks, Pete." Charlie moved back toward the doorway. "I don't think we're going to surprise anyone now."

"Hold it!" Kerry grabbed Charlie's coat. "What's that?"

"Where?"

"Over there!"

A rat scurried over a pile of chains on the deck.

"Looks like a rat to me." Charlie tried to keep his tense voice from cracking. "I'm not turning back now."

The foursome filed through the doorway. At the bottom of the stairs they studied the darkness for any sign of light. They could barely see shadows in the hallway.

"There! Over there!" Laura grabbed Charlie's shoulders and pointed him toward a light shining under a door.

"Somebody's here," Pete whispered.

"Ahhhhhhhh." The sound echoed in the passage. Cold chills raced through each of them.

Without a word all four raced for the stairs and stumbled toward the deck. Never looking back they bounded for the side and scurried down the ladder.

Pete was the first to reach the boat. He started untying the rope while Kerry pushed it away from the ship. Panting, Laura jumped the last few feet with Charlie leaping behind her.

"Row, Kerry, row!" Pete shouted.

"Watch the ship in case anyone starts shooting at us," Charlie said.

With eyes wide open they all stared until they had floated far enough away to relax.

"That was terrific!" Charlie said gleefully. "Talk about adventure!"

"I'm glad you liked it, Charlie," Kerry said. "From now on, I'll get my adventure from Saturday morning cartoons."

"Don't you understand?" Charlie persisted. "We proved it. Someone does live on that ship. No one has proved that except us. How exciting can life get?"

"Wrong, crab breath," Kerry said. "We only proved there is noise on that ship. There might be a sea monster, or maybe it's haunted or something."

"Don't get carried away," Charlie argued. "You've been watching the Midnight Monster Movie too often. We have to think this through. Then we can begin to plan our return to the ship."

"Return?" Pete gulped.

"Sorry, I'm expecting a broken leg that night," retorted Kerry.

"You really are crazy, Charlie," Laura began

putting her crab bait away. "But the truth is, you do some daring things. You plan it and I'll come back with you. After all, a girl isn't frightened by a little noise."

Fishing with his father was one of Charlie's favorite sports. For hours they would sit and talk about the Bay, its riches, its past and its future. Charlie didn't think anyone knew more about it than his dad did.

"You seem quiet this evening." Mr. Dean pulled at his rod, but felt no bite.

"Oh, it's nothing. I might be a little tired. I don't need to go to bed earlier, though; I'm just tired."

"Everybody gets that way. Look over there. That fellow is patent-tonging. A pretty good way to catch oysters. That hoist and pulley make it a lot easier. The guys who tong by hand strain their backs every day."

Mr. Dean had grown up on the Bay and had never considered living anywhere else. He managed a cannery and felt good about raising his family near the water.

"If I ever do it"—Charlie put new bait on his hook—"I'll *dive* for oysters. That's the best yet. Do you remember oyster wars on the Bay?"

"Sure. Not the worst time—that was back around 1880. But I can remember 1959. The last killing over oysters was probably then."

"That would have been fun to be an oyster policeman and chase boats, with pistols blazing."

"It was just that way, too. Watermen would jump from one boat to a faster one to get away from the speeding police. They had boats hiding in the marsh to help them escape."

"Were oysters that big a business?"

"In the 1880's watermen took fifteen million bushels of oysters out of here. At the turn of the century the annual catch had dwindled to three million. Now they say the industry might be in danger."

"Hey, Dad," said Charlie, pointing out into space, "Is that a hawk?"

"I don't think so. I wish I had my binoculars. It looks like it could be a bald eagle."

"Right here on the Bay?"

"Sure. There used to be plenty of eagles, too. That's probably how the eagle became our national bird. There used to be lots of eagles in this area."

"What happened to them?"

"Most people think DDT finished them off. About ten years ago, DDT was outlawed around here, and now the eagle is coming back. It makes you feel good; to an eagle, it gives hope for tomorrow."

Mr. Dean pulled up the collar on his jacket to fight off the evening chill.

"Have you ever heard about the crab that throws hand grenades?" Charlie knew his dad was a good listener.

"Can't say I have." Mr. Dean began to wind up his reel.

"It lives in the Indian Ocean—it has some long name. Anyway, it doesn't have very strong claws to defend itself, so it carries a sea anemone in each claw. Those babies are alive and can really sting. When an enemy comes, the crab throws one of those creatures like a hand grenade. If it hits, it can give a terrible sting. It makes everything want to stay clear."

Mr. Dean took the oars. "There aren't any of those in the Bay, are there?"

"No, the blue crabs here have strong enough claws;

they don't need hand grenades."

Charlie moved up next to his dad and took one of the oars. They sat together and sliced the oars into the water and headed for home.

As they rowed, Charlie felt a grin inside. He held it there because he didn't want to look silly. He loved having a father he could talk to.

Chapter Three

"Will you quit whining, Pete? Mom and Dad will never know we were on the ship. So cool it."

"I wish someone would help me row this crate," Kerry complained. His back bowed with each thrust through the water.

"Why did you bring a flashlight in the daytime?" Pete asked, hugging Throckmorton.

"Why did you bring a beagle in a rowboat?" Laura snapped. "There are dark corners in ships even during the day, Oyster Brain."

"Stop bickering. We have to work together or we'll end up in trouble," Charlie warned. "Old ships probably have loose floors and doors swinging on hinges. . . . "

"And old hermits," Laura added.

"Don't worry." Charlie assured. "There isn't anything on that ship that we can't handle." He took the rope and stood ready to tie it to the ship's ladder.

"Step lively!" Charlie ordered as he pulled himself up onto the first rung. He carried a wooden mallet in one hand.

"You look really dumb with that football helmet on, Kerry," Laura said disgustedly.

"It pays to be prepared." Kerry picked up an oar and carried it up the ladder. Laura thought for barely a second and then grabbed the second oar.

Pete hustled up the ladder with a small fishing net draped over his shoulder.

When they arrived on the deck the quartet stood close together; none looked relaxed. Eight wide eyes searched the ship for any sign of movement. No one seemed anxious to walk far from their only escape route.

"This is really stupid, Charlie," Laura said weakly. "How'd I let you talk me into this?"

"What if we get jumped or something?" Kerry asked.

"I've got a plan, don't worry," Charlie explained. "Everybody grab the belt of the person in front of you. That way we can't be separated. I'll watch straight ahead. Kerry, you watch right; Laura, you look left; Pete, you keep an eye on the rear."

"All together, let's head for the stairs."

They shuffled across the deck like a dragon in a Chinese New Year parade. Heads bobbed in all directions, oars stood erect like flags and Charlie's right arm was thrust forward with his wooden hammer, ready to do battle.

Squeezing through the doorway was just the beginning of their troubles. The steep, narrow stairs weren't made for a cluster of people.

"You must have oatmeal for brains," Laura whispered.

Charlie pulled forward. "Knock it off. Don't let go of those belts."

Like toothpaste, they inched down the stairs until they reached the floor below. Their eyes moved around like frightened kittens.

Kerry pointed with his oar. "That's the door that had the light."

"Ahhhhhhhh!" A terrible scream rang through the ship.

The four turned and bolted for the stairs, all arriving at the same time. They tumbled into a heap—legs, oars and net flying in all directions. Pete's net wrapped around Kerry's helmeted head. Squirming and tripping over each other, they failed to gain their footing.

"He's going to kill us all," Laura moaned.

"Quiet!" Charlie hissed. "Straighten up. No one is going to kill us. Let go of my leg, Kerry!"

"Let's get out of here," Pete insisted.

"This is no time to turn chicken." Charlie struggled to his feet. "What if someone is lying in there wounded or dying? We can't just leave him."

"I'm no hero," Kerry adjusted his helmet.

"Ahhhhhhhh!" The scream sent chills through them.

"D-don't—d-don't—d-don't let that scare you." Charlie's throat sounded hoarse. "Let's stick to our original plan. Grab each other's belt."

"I haven't even written a will," said Pete as he folded his net and took a firm hold on Laura's belt.

"This would go a lot better if I led," said Laura, grabbing Charlie's belt. "Girls have a way of being level-headed—firm, but sensible."

"Girls have a way of being noisy! Follow me."

"Ahhhhhhhh!"

The group jerked to a stop.

"Forward," Charlie's voice cracked.

They shuffled to the door. Cautiously, Charlie reached out his left hand and turned the knob. The narrow door swung open to show an amazing sight.

"It looks like a fancy junkyard," Laura said.

"Look at those huge balls of string!" Kerry exclaimed.

"And piles of old newspapers," Pete added.

"Stay together," Charlie commanded.

They inched inside.

"Ahhhhhhhh!"

Chills shook their spines.

"That scream isn't coming from in here," Charlie said, and reached out to take a silver candleholder from the shelf. "Look at these beauties."

SLAM!

They all knew what the sound meant, but they were too afraid to turn. The room was quieter than a flea tiptoeing on cotton.

"Well, it looks like I have company," a raspy voice crackled.

"Turning to face the sound, they saw a gray-haired man no more than five feet tall, with a long white beard and yellow teeth. Their eyes dropped to the old musket he held in his hand.

"Allow me to introduce myself. I am Captain Arnold K. Rankin—and *you* are trespassing."

"Ahhhhhhhh!" the scream echoed.

"Wh-wh-who is doing that screaming?" Charlie's words choked out.

"Never you mind." The hermit tossed the musket into his left hand. "That may be too horrible for you to know about. Now give me a reason why I shouldn't shoot all of you and feed you to the crabs."

"This wasn't my idea, Captain Rankin." Kerry let go of the belt he was holding. "I didn't even want to come. Why don't I just slip quietly back to the boat?"

"Stand still and rest your oars on the floor. Hee, Hee, Hee!" Captain Rankin's screechy laugh raised the hair on the back of everyone's necks.

"Let's just talk, Captain," Laura said calmly. "We are really your friends."

"How can you be my friends when you don't know me?"

"But we are," she argued. "I'd like to know all about your room—like this guitar with only one string. Do you play it?"

"Ahhhhhhhh!"

Everyone's face cringed.

"Sit down, all of you. Don't move and I'll put an end to all that screaming."

"Put an end to it?" Charlie gulped.

"Don't worry, I'll be right back. Hee, Hee, Hee!"

The hermit disappeared in a second. Laura and Charlie looked at each other wondering whether or not to break for the door. Pete started to rise to his feet.

"Hold it." The Captain popped back through the door. "Thought about running, didn't you? I would have mowed you down in the hallway. Hee, Hee, Hee!"

He tossed the musket to his right hand, and then back to his left like a child with a toy. Pulling at his beard, Captain Rankin's flashing eyes kept everyone nervous.

"I really like your silver candlesticks." Charlie pointed to the eight, standing side-by-side.

"Is *that* why you came?" His voice was now harsh. "Someone sent you for the candlesticks, didn't they? Now I'm going to have to drill you. Hee, Hee, Hee!"

Sweat seemed to mount on their foreheads everytime he laughed and tossed the musket.

"Who sent you? Who sent you?"

"No one sent us," Charlie insisted. "We just like your candlesticks."

"They're *mine*. The other four are mine, too, and I'm going to get them. There were a dozen of them, you know."

"Well, maybe we could help you get them. Who has the other four? We could go talk to him—or her."

"Would you really help me? They wouldn't be easy to get, you know. Hee, Hee, Hee! I had to steal back these eight."

Captain Rankin lowered himself slowly to the floor and sat cross-legged.

"I came to the Bay just six years ago. Had nothing to my name but twelve silver candlesticks."

As he spoke, his face grew taut with anger. His left eye started to twitch.

"That's all I had to my name."

"Where—where did you get the candlesticks?" Laura asked, almost afraid to interrupt.

"I made them," the captain barked back, "with my own hands." There was no laugh left in his voice. "See these rough knuckles?" He lifted his free hand toward the motionless children. "They're crafty little beggars. Can fix about anything, and can make things quicker than lightning."

"I came here trusting everybody and thinking I could get a fair wage for my work."

Kerry shook everytime the captain's eye twitched.

"But I'm no fool." Captain Rankin raised his musket to Charlie's eye level. "I'll track down every one of those candleholders, because they're mine. I'll get them back. And if I have to, I'll handle that crook who stole them.

"And if I have to, I'll point this worn old musket at that crook's head and, as sure as I'm a clam eater, I'll squeeze this trigger and—BOOM!"

Charlie gasped and grabbed his throat. Laura hit her head on the steel wall behind her. Kerry screamed—he felt embarrassed that he had screamed. Pete only whimpered.

"Don't let me frighten you. Hee, Hee, Hee!" His twitch had stopped. "I just want to leave this old ship and head back home to Kentucky."

"How can you find out who has the candlesticks?" Charlie asked.

"I sneak into jewelry stores and go through their receipts. I don't steal anything—I'm no thief. I just take back what is mine."

"Sir, I think we can help you," Charlie forced his warmest smile. "You let us go and we promise to help you find the last four candlesticks."

"That would be better than shooting you and feeding you to the crabs. Hee, Hee, Hee!"

Laura stood up. "No doubt about it. We've worked together as detectives before. We do slick work."

"All right. But if you doublecross me, you'll feel the fire from this old musket. Hee, Hee, Hee!"

He told them the names of the three jewelry stores that had sold the candlesticks. Because of his appearance and strange laugh, most people refused to talk to him, so he resorted to sneaking around at night. Some of the candlesticks had been sold four or five times and by now were hard to trace.

After discussing candlesticks, they talked about the odd objects in the room. The Captain had a large box of bird feathers. Some were beautiful, white sea gull feathers and others were short and frizzy.

The ball of string was nearly three feet high. He had never thrown a piece away.

One wall was almost completely covered with cigar

bands pasted tightly against each other. Another wall had pictures of lion heads torn from magazines.

A small camp stove and a pile of dishes made up his kitchen. Crackers and cheese were all the food they could see.

"We had better go now," Kerry suggested. "It must be getting dark."

Charlie patted the man gently on the back. "But we will get back to you soon."

"Oh, not too quick. Wait here." The Captain hustled out the door.

"Ahhhhhhhh!"

The terrible scream had returned and it had lost none of its horror. The Captain again stood in the doorway. "Just so you won't forget who you are dealing with." He grinned.

They had never been so glad to see Throckmorton. Piling into the boat, they untied and pushed off.

"That was great thinking. Fantastic!" Kerry pulled the oars briskly. "Giving him that line about coming back to help him was pure genius."

"It did the job all right. It got us out of there," Laura agreed.

"You've got it all wrong." Charlie slumped down on the seat. "It was no line. We *have* to come back. We *have* to help."

"You're crazy!" Laura blurted.

"If you do, you go without me," Kerry announced. "Why do I always have to row this thing?"

VVVROOM, VVVROOM!

Charlie revved the engine on his go-cart. Each time he pulled the throttle lever, it roared like a jet.

As he walked around the cart, Charlie felt his chest swell with pride. The red paint and glistening silver hubcaps were as glamorous as any Mercedes Charlie had ever seen. He had sprayed gold glitter on the steering wheel and upholstered the seat with slick black leather from a chair he had bought at a garage sale.

VVVROOM, VVVROOM!

He loved to hear that sound. Carefully, he greased its steering joints and packed some in around the steering wheel bracket.

Charlie's parents weren't as happy with the cart as their son. It left terrible tracks in the backyard, moved at a frightening speed and always made a deafening noise. Charlie wondered if he would enjoy being an adult. They didn't like noise, video games, soda drinking contests, mud fights, low grades, dirty jeans or messy rooms. He had promised himself to like all of these when he grew up.

When Laura and Kerry arrived, Charlie was eager to start.

Laura warned, "This time, don't start until we say ready." She began climbing the branches of a huge tree. "Hand them to me one box at a time."

Kerry lifted a box of water balloons while Charlie adjusted his helmet.

"When you give the signal I'll take off," Charlie said, wiggling into the leather seat. He shoved the throttle and roared off.

Laura wedged the first box onto a limb and pushed the second box one branch higher. When Kerry was safely by her side, they looked to the north end of the yard to find Charlie. He was perched on a slight ridge, engine revving, hands locked on the golden wheel.

Charlie waved the signal.

"One!" called Laura.

"Two!"

"Three!"

Lurching forward, the go-cart careened across the yard. Kerry and Laura steadied their water balloons waiting for the target to race under them.

"Now!" Laura shouted, and two balloons dropped like rocks.

The red balloon smashed across Charlie's right front tire, but the blue one crashed behind him. Without a word he circled and sped back to his starting position.

VVVROOM, VVVROOM!

"Don't tell me when to drop them," Kerry scolded, and pulled a large yellow balloon from the box. "You made me miss."

"Made you miss?" Laura held a second red bomb in her hand. "Let's see you hit it this time, Mr. Ace Marksman."

Raising his hand to signal them, Charlie's smile stretched ear to ear. Under the rules he could be the driver until a balloon hit his body. Feet and legs did not count, but hands, head, chest and arms did. Whoever hit him became the new driver. He could swirl the go-cart, but had to go under the tree.

A second time Charlie raced under his attackers and balloons came crashing down. The first hit his left foot and a second splattered behind the leather seat.

Charlie hurried back to his starting point.

VVVROOM, VVVROOM!

Rocking and bouncing, the go-cart lunged forward again. As it neared the tree, Kerry straightened up to get into position. His left elbow jerked back and hit a box of balloons, sending it tumbling from the branch.

With perfect timing, the balloons landed squarely on Charlie's head, completely blocking his vision. The balloons burst, soaking him.

Unable to see, Charlie continued full speed ahead toward his mother's clothesline. As he crashed through the sheets hanging on the line, one tore loose and covered Charlie, box, go-cart and all. The right wheels climbed onto a pile of boards, dumping the cart on its left side. Charlie rolled out and tried to struggle to his feet. His left hand dropped into a can of grease.

Laura pulled the sheet from the mummy and Kerry helped Charlie move the go-cart off the box. They all laughed like hyenas—except Charlie.

"I thought you weren't going out for basketball," Charlie said, and dropped his gym bag on the bench in front of a row of lockers.

"When I heard you were going out, I decided it must be easy," Kerry answered, pulling the strings tightly on his basketball shoes. "If you dribble like you drive a go-cart, you'll never get to play."

"Just forget about the go-cart. Is this locker empty?" Charlie started to unbutton his shirt. "Stay around after practice. I want to talk to you about that ship."

"No thanks. My family is suffering from leprosy and I have to stay home and nurse them back to health."

"I've got a foolproof plan to help the guy. I'll tell you about it later."

"Don't strain your imagination just for me. I joined the Foreign Legion. I have to leave for North Africa right after practice."

"If you don't quit yapping, I'm going to cut you out of the plan." Charlie pulled his trunks out of the bag.

"It sounds like a cruel punishment, but please cut me out."

"You'll change your mind. What's this? You are reading *Stock Investments*?" Charlie reached for one of Kerry's books.

"Never mind," Kerry pulled the book back.

"Let me see it. You can't be reading *Stock Investments*."

"Will you keep it a secret?"

"Fine!"

"It isn't really a book—look at this."

Kerry pointed to a small, black lid at the top. He unscrewed it.

"It's really a flask." Kerry lifted the book and drank out of the top. "It holds a pint of soda and no one can figure it out." He turned it up for another drink.

Charlie smiled. "Sometimes you do come up with good ideas."

Chapter Four

Mr. Dean offered to take Charlie and his friends to Sandy Point for Chesapeake Appreciation Days. They went every year. It was more fun than a carnival or circus. The plan was to leave at ten o'clock and come back late. This gave Charlie barely one hour to get his job done in town before leaving for Sandy Point.

Laura and Charlie parked their bikes outside the jewelry shop and hurried inside. Trying to look casual, they strolled slowly by the counters. After a few minutes the salesman walked over to them.

"How can I help you two today? Not looking for a diamond, are you?" He chuckled.

"We're sort of window shopping," Charlie said haltingly as he gazed around.

Before anyone could say another word the door opened and a tall man entered. He was wearing a dark blue coat with the collar turned up. His tan felt hat was pulled down tightly. Despite a week-old growth of whiskers, a wide scar still showed through on the left side of his chin.

"Do you carry any candleholders?" Charlie asked.

"Certainly. We have them gold plated, silver plated and in sterling silver. Let me show you some."

The salesman placed several pair on the counter. "Of course, the sterling ones are antique and sell at $500 apiece. The plated ones are much—"

"Tell me more about the sterling ones," Charlie interrupted. He couldn't ignore the fact that they looked exactly like the ones he had seen on the ship.

"Suppose I would buy one of these as a special gift for my mother. Do they hold their value over the years, or is their price going up?" Charlie questioned.

"No problem. Right now their value is excellent."

"We might feel better if you would check something for us." Laura pressed against the counter. "Would you look at a couple of old sales receipts and tell us how much they were—compared to now?"

"Well, I don't know. I don't usually—"

"It would just take a few minutes and we would feel a lot better." Laura gave him her best nice-young-lady smile.

In a minute he was back with a stack of receipts and began rifling through them.

"Here's one I sold only three months ago. It sold for $475. Let's see—this one earlier was $450. You can see they're going up in price regularly."

Charlie started to leave. "Thanks a lot!"

"We'll talk about it," said Laura.

The man in the tan hat had just left the store.

"There has been a great deal of interest in silver candlesticks lately. The rough-looking man who just left was asking about these, also. And there have been many stolen in recent years."

"Thank you," Charlie said. "So long."

Outside Charlie and Laura stopped. "Quick, Laura! A piece of paper. Write down 1112 Logan Avenue."

"And 6804 Perch Road," Laura added. "We've got both addresses."

They climbed on their bicycles and pedaled for

home with the first leg of their mission accomplished.

The man in the tan hat stepped out from the shadows and grabbed a bicycle from the stand in front of the supermarket. Cautiously he followed them.

When Laura and Charlie arrived at Collins Landing, Mr. Dean was packed and ready to go. The station wagon pulled out of the drive with Charlie and Pete in the front seat and Kerry and Laura in the back. As they picked up speed no one noticed a man in a tan hat, riding a bicycle.

They drove through St. Michaels, took the bypass around Easton and moved north on Route 50 toward the Chesapeake Bay Bridge. Laura brought her Rubik's Cube along and a booklet telling her what moves to make. She had no trouble matching the colors on one side—red was her favorite, but the rest was pure jungle.

"Bet you don't know how an oyster gets around," Charlie called out from the front seat.

Pete was playing with the radio dial. "Don't tell me it takes the subway."

"They don't get around." Kerry declared, leaning forward. "After they settle on a shell, they just sit still until a waterman finds them."

"Almost!" Charlie replied. "Actually, they do have a small foot when they are young. They stick it out of their shell and push around on the Bay floor. When they get older, the foot just disappears."

"Fascinating." Laura didn't bother to look up. "I'll bet the whole world is waiting to learn that."

"You really hate to learn, don't you?" Charlie growled. "Facts probably give you a headache."

"I enjoy *useful* facts, but stories about oyster feet

44

don't exactly grab me." Laura gave the cube a couple of extra twists.

"Then I have a 'useful' fact for you. It will probably come in handy some day. Did you know that ants are used in surgery?"

"This has to be a joke," said Kerry, who was now watching the Canada geese flying over.

"No joke," Charlie declared. "In parts of South America they use the Eciton ants in surgery. If you have a deep cut, a modern doctor might use ants to close the wound."

"Charlie, I think the putty is coming loose in your skull," Laura chirped.

"They pick up the ant and hold it over the wound. Then they squeeze its body." Charlie demonstrated with his hands. "The ant bites the skin making the wound come together. Then the doctor snaps the ant's body off."

"Sick," Laura groaned.

"The ant's head stays in place until the cut heals. Then the doctor simply removes the head."

"That's the most disgusting story I've ever heard," Laura insisted.

"I think it's neat," Pete grinned.

"I think it's a bunch of baloney," Kerry concluded.

"That's what happens when I hang around with people who can't read."

Mr. Dean smiled, but decided not to get involved.

Their day at Sandy Point was nothing short of spectacular. Broad, white sails stretched taut against the wind as many different boats crowded into the area. Charlie and his friends thrilled at the skipjack races as the old oyster dredgers sliced across the water. It was a cool afternoon, but the wide open sun felt good, gently baking all their faces.

The sky divers caught Charlie's imagination. They dropped through the air for several minutes before opening their parachutes. To fall that freely and then to land exactly on target was one of the most exciting things he had ever seen. Charlie made a mental note to do that someday.

No less amazing were the hang gliders. Like giant kites they arched through the air with their gorgeous colors splashed against a blue sky.

Laura exclaimed, "Fantabulous," as she peered through her sunglasses. "Now you're talking about a sport. Forget basketball, I want to hang glide."

At noon they enjoyed a selection of oysters. Charlie ate two raw oysters, more out of dare than pleasure. However, they all liked fried oyster fritter sandwiches. Kerry gulped two bowls of hot oyster soup. The smell of oysters cooking made their mouths water, and they ate like cub bears waking in the spring.

No matter what was on the menu, Pete's favorite was always a soda. It didn't have to be cold. He could down three or four warm root beers as if he were sampling mints.

Each had his hands stuffed with food as they watched the oyster shucking contest. At almost lightning speed, the participants would pry open an oyster with a short knife, scrape the shell clean and dump the empty shell into a basket. Shucking is nearly an art on the Chesapeake Bay. The contestants had years of experience and considerable skill. The winner was a quick-wristed woman. She lived near Cambridge and claimed she had been shucking for nearly thirty years.

Charlie and Laura took their time strolling through the art and photo exhibits lined up inside a huge white tent.

"Next year I should bring some pictures down here," Charlie thought aloud. "Never know, but I might pick up a prize."

"Just don't bring any green monster photos," Laura reminded him. "You know, the kind you make up from toys."

"Don't you ever forget anything?"

"I told you I wasn't going back out to that ship."

"Don't talk so much, Kerry," Charlie insisted. "Just keep rowing. We can't abandon Captain Rankin."

"I've got to get a new set of friends," Laura said, as she held the rope ready to tie up at the ship. "This crew gets into the weirdest fixes."

"You head up first, Pete," Charlie called out.

"You bet." Pete grabbed the first rung and pulled himself up. As his foot hit the rung, it slipped on the moisture and he fell. But his elastic belt caught on a rusty edge of the ladder and held him in the air. Like a yo-yo, Pete bounced slightly, feet dangling loosely.

"Grab him!" Kerry shouted.

Charlie took two quick steps toward Pete, but lost his balance, tripped over the seat and tumbled overboard.

"Help!" Charlie shouted from the cold water.

"Help!" Pete yelled as he tried to regain his footing on the slippery, wobbling ladder.

"You grab Pete!" Laura called, and dashed to the side of the boat to help Charlie.

Kerry cried, "Get Charlie!" Dropping his oars, he lunged for the suspended Pete.

Kerry threw his arms around Pete while Laura took Charlie's hand. With one huge thrust Kerry lifted Pete high enough to free his belt.

"Got it." Kerry sounded proud. He then stumbled backwards two steps and tripped over the port side with Pete roosting high in his arms.

Splash! They hit the water like wounded whales.

Mumbling and groaning, the three soaked boys finally struggled back into the boat. As each climbed in, the craft rocked briskly from side to side. They sat for a minute shivering and disgusted.

"You all look like drowned chickens," Laura said impatiently, then clucked and flapped her arms at the miserable boys.

"This is probably not the time to mention this, but you should notice that this does seem to be a boy problem. You klutzes are the ones that dumped into the drink. You didn't see *me* stumbling around and falling over the side."

Silently the boys stared stonefaced at Laura.

"Maybe this is the time to consider having a girl as a leader. Joan of Arc didn't do all that badly in France. The only reason they burned her was jealousy."

The boys began to show their teeth. Charlie was making snarling sounds like a dog.

"Well, I can see you aren't in a mood for discussing new ideas. Why don't we just drop the matter and head up the ladder. I'll be happy to go—"

All three boys sprang from their seats and grabbed Laura.

"This isn't funny!" Kicking and screaming, Laura tried to fight back as they lifted her into the air.

"One." They started to swing their squirming victim.

"I'm going to tell!"

"Two."

"Men don't do this to women!"

"Three."

The girl arched slightly into the air and dropped like a bomb into the Bay. A large splash rose up as the three boys forced themselves to laugh as hard as they could.

"All four of you look a bit soggy. Hee, Hee, Hee." Mr. Rankin handed each of them a tattered blanket to wrap around their shoulders. They sat close to the small stove in the center of the room.

Charlie tried to find a comfortable position, but his wet jeans made it impossible. "Don't you get lonely on this ship?" he asked.

"I'm not alone. There's someone in the other room."

"You mean that terrible scream we heard?" Kerry asked. He accepted a cracker from the hermit.

"Never you mind about the next room." Captain Rankin's eyes widened. "It might be someone—or some*thing*." His words had an eerie sound. "It could be almost anything—even a ghost. Hee, Hee, Hee."

All four of them felt chills shiver up their backs— and not just from the dampness.

"Besides, I have other friends. Octavia is my best friend. Do you want to meet Octavia? Come on, get up, follow me. Hee, Hee, Hee."

As they walked past the mysterious door, each listened for sounds. There was no screaming this time. In their imaginations they tried to picture what gruesome sight might be in there.

"Stand over there. I don't want you scaring Octavia. Hee, Hee, Hee."

The Captain ambled over to the barrel on the deck and removed the lid. Removing three large oysters, he pried them open and placed each carefully on the steel railing. The raw oysters and half shells glistened in the setting sun.

"Don't move a hair on your head or wiggle an eyebrow—or Octavia won't come."

"How long does it take before this Octavia usually shows up?" Charlie asked after waiting several minutes. "I think I'm catching pneumonia out here."

"Most often it's right away. Other times I've waited an hour. Hee, Hee, Hee."

Five more minutes felt like hours as a cool breeze swept across the wet onlookers. Laura's wet hair was matted into lumps where curls had once been.

"It's Octavia! It's Octavia!" Captain Rankin whispered excitedly.

A large, beautiful, white sea gull lowered itself onto the railing. Most sea gulls looked similar, but this one seemed to have a broader chest and an air of dignity that lifted it above others.

Octavia snapped an oyster off its shell and artfully rose back into the sky.

"That's Octavia. She'll come back later to eat the others, too."

"And Octavia is your friend?" Kerry asked.

"My *best* friend. If you hadn't been here I would have walked over to the rail and talked to her. Sea gulls know a lot—and they can keep secrets. Hee, Hee, Hee!"

Back inside, they sat cross-legged and watched Mr. Rankin's amazing face. His cheeks, twitching eyes and dancing forehead put special emphasis on his every word.

Charlie asked, "What would you say if I told you

we have found the other silver candlesticks?"

"I'd tell you they are mine. All twelve were mine. I was going to sell them, but they were stolen from me. I'll get the other four; you watch."

"But you can't go on stealing," Laura declared. "Someday you'll get caught and they'll put you in jail."

"I can't steal what is really mine. I found the other eight in people's homes. It took me years. At night I would look in windows around the Bay. When I found one, I'd break in and take it—nothing else, mind you—just my candlesticks."

"It sounds impossible to find those," Charlie said.

"It sounds that way, but, I'm patient, and clever too. I only go ashore Mondays, Wednesdays and Fridays. If I go every night, they'll catch me. Nobody's going to catch me."

"If you could prove they're stolen, the police would help you get them back." Charlie suggested. He pulled his blanket tightly around his shoulders.

"Can't prove it. It just happened. I was showing them to a man and he pulled a gun on me and took them. A big, ugly fellow—had a terrible scar on the left side of his face."

"We'd hate to see you go to jail," Laura said compassionately. "Who would take care of Octavia?"

"You worry too much. I'm not going anywhere and I'll get my candlesticks back. Hee, Hee, Hee."

"We promised to help you, Captain Rankin," Charlie assured, "and we will. We'll figure out an *honest* way to get those back."

"Excuse me." The Captain bounced up and left the room. In less than a minute he returned.

"I'm afraid you'd better go. My friend in the other room is starting to feel bad."

"Ahhhhhhhh!" The horrible scream bellowed from the next door.

All four children could feel themselves stiffen with the terrible sound.

"You be sure and come again. Hee, Hee, Hee."

"Can't we meet your friend before we go?" Charlie asked unsteadily.

"Not now. Besides, it isn't so easy to meet a ghost. Hee, Hee, Hee."

"Ahhhhhhhh!"

Chapter Five

Woody's General Store looked a little like Captain Rankin's room, except it was clean and neat. Crabbing nets hung high on the walls, boxes of boots were stacked near the pot-bellied stove, cases of motor oil and fresh bait were along the wall. There was a soda can machine, and a rectangular metal cooler filled with ice and water and bottles of soda.

There were two small tables with chairs. One held a checkerboard where men played the game by the hour. The second table was for eating sandwiches and cupcakes, and drinking soda. Charlie, Kerry and Laura sat there to discuss important matters.

"That's a lousy idea," Kerry said, as he took a big drink of red cream soda.

"It's a brilliant idea," Charlie protested. "We buy the last four candleholders and give them to the captain. Then we talk him into moving to a nice rest home where people can take care of him."

Laura unwrapped a chocolate cupcake. "Sure, and all we need is two thousand dollars."

"That is a problem. Maybe we can sell some things."

"Two thousand bucks, Charlie." Laura's voice rose. "We aren't talking your basic twenty dollars. Besides, there are a few things you seem to forget. The most important one being that scream coming from the other room. There could be some guy dying in there."

"No chance. I've got that one figured out. Rankin has a sick friend in there. Or else he has a friend who is pretending to be sick."

Kerry took another big swig. "What if it's a ghost? My mom says there are a lot of ghosts around the Bay."

"I can't believe this." Charlie groaned and dropped his head into his arms on the table. "You and your mom."

"There's many a waterman who has gone down in the Bay and his body has never been found. They say the crabs get their bodies, but their souls never find rest. They just walk around the Bay forever."

"Why am I sitting here?" Laura asked. "On the one side, I have a guy who thinks money gushes out of toothpaste tubes and on the other, I have a guy who believes in the bogeyman."

"You don't have to believe it, but some night you just listen to things moving in the bushes," Kerry dared.

Charlie didn't bother to lift his head. "I think they call that *wind*, Kerry."

"Well, laugh if you want, but I'm not going into that room."

"Plus," Laura jumped in, "you keep forgetting the other big problem, Charlie. Your parents said you can't go on the ship."

"And what solution do you have, Wonder Woman?"

"It's simple. We call the police and let them handle it."

"That's what I like about you, Laura; you have

jellyfish legs. You don't care about the Captain's feelings. Go ahead. Crush the old man."

Woody walked over to listen in.

"I don't know what this is all about, but you sound pretty excited."

"It's hopeless, Woody," Laura replied. "It's like trying to put a Band-Aid on Charlie's head when what he really needs is a brain transplant."

"Yeah," Kerry added, "you don't know where we can get a good, used oyster brain, do you?"

"I've got a great idea for you, Woody," Charlie announced. "You ought to put some electronic games in your store. You'll make a mint. Get a Donkey Kong or a Pac-Man. Kids will line up to play them."

"It's nice of you to think about me, but I'm not sure I need all that noise," Woody smiled. "When it's quiet like this, people feel free to talk."

"What do you hear about fishing?" Charlie asked, changing the subject again.

"Not too much. The big rockfish are moving toward the center of the Bay where it's warmer."

"How big do these rockfish get?"

"Quite large. Some are 6 feet long and weigh 175 pounds or more."

"That big in the Bay?" Kerry marveled.

"Sure, and there'll be more of them if we have enough sense to keep the Bay clean and not overuse it."

Soon Charlie, Kerry and Laura left the warm stove and began their walk home in the early dusk.

"Let's meet tomorrow after basketball practice," Charlie suggested. "Then we can start to put our plan into action."

"I'll meet with you, but it all sounds boneheaded to me," Kerry said, as he pushed his hands into his pockets.

"Keep looking ahead and talk normal," Laura whispered sternly. "There's a man behind us with a tan hat. He looks like he's following us. He gives me the creeps."

"It's your imagination," Charlie scoffed. "Between you and Kerry, I'm going to start seeing things. Just in case you are right, let's lose this guy. At the corner by the grocery, let's split."

The trio began walking faster. The man in the tan hat increased his speed. Faster. Faster. At the corner Kerry turned left and Laura right.

The man stopped for a minute and looked in all three directions. Quickly he made up his mind and continued to trail Charlie.

Charlie took a glance back and increased his pace. Walking as fast as he could, Charlie decided he would head toward the woods. It was dark enough to make it hard to follow anyone.

The next time Charlie looked back he saw Laura and Kerry coming out of the grocery store. Each carried something and they were jogging behind the man. When the man looked behind to see who was coming, Charlie dashed into the woods.

Unsure what to do, the man looked both ways and decided to plunge into the woods after Charlie. Hearing a noise in the brush, he hurried in that direction.

Snap! Snap! He heard twigs break behind. The man pivoted and raced toward the noise. Snap! Snap! He grinned slightly as he walked to a large tree and slowly began to look around it.

Fsssst! White shaving cream shot across his eyes

from the can Laura was holding. The man yelled and grabbed for his eyes. He turned around, wiping the cream from his face. Fsssst! Kerry caught him with a second shot.

"You bunch of brats!" The man swung with his fist, but couldn't see well enough to hit anyone. He swung again.

Fsssst! Fsssst! Every time he began to wipe some away, another shot frosted his eyes. He spun in a circle throwing punches in every direction. As he turned, his legs hit against a fallen tree and he tripped face first over the log.

Unsatisfied, Laura and Kerry shook the cans hard and prepared to give him more of the same.

"Hold it!" Laura warned Kerry.

The blinded man had reached into his coat and pulled out a revolver. Laura and Kerry bounded through the woods, leaping over logs and zig-zagging around trees.

"Bang!" A shot rang out as they joined Charlie and tore out of the forest.

"Something tells me I shouldn't interrupt two great thinkers like you. I think I'll head inside—youth group's starting in a minute." Laura looked sharp in her yellow jacket and brown skirt. "By the way, did you guys tell your parents about Robin Hood and his pistol?"

Charlie didn't bother to turn around. "No way."

"If I did, my mother would really be burned." Kerry spit toward a rock. "We probably should, though. Somebody's going to get killed—us."

"What are you mud-heads doing?"

"We are doing boys' things, so just move on." Charlie spit toward the target.

"You're spitting? Now that's a big-boy thing. I'll bet when the Baltimore Colts get together, they all stand around and spit."

Charlie spit again. "Will you take a hike?"

"I hear it's part of basic training in the Marine Corps. They spend a whole week learning to spit like men."

"You don't understand anything," Charlie growled. "We're spitting through our teeth. It's something girls can't do."

"Oh, pardon me. I wish guys would teach girls to spit through their teeth. Then they could include it in the Miss America contest. Right after the talent finals they could hold the spit-off challenge. 'And now Miss New Jersey will spit 25 yards and make it do a double flip.'"

Charlie's forehead wrinkled as he stared humorlessly at Laura.

"Okay! Okay! I'll bug off." Laura tried to calm Charlie down. "I'll just go inside for youth group."

"Now that's thinking," Charlie agreed.

"I'm going, I'm going."

"Then go."

"So long," she replied, stepping backwards.

"Go!"

Laura stopped backing up. "Just one suggestion."

"Good grief," Charlie grunted.

"Why don't you let a weak little girl try spitting through her teeth? Just once."

"That sounds fair to me," Kerry conceded.

"Stay out of this," Charlie retorted through clenched teeth.

"One try won't hurt," Laura coaxed.

"All right, all right. Just one try. Stand here and don't cross this line." Charlie made a mark in the dirt with his foot. "The target is that rock. You get one shot."

Laura toed the mark and looked across to the rock.

"You wouldn't want to suck a lemon before you start would you? A nice, *sour* lemon," Charlie teased.

"Keep quiet," Laura snapped.

"Make sure it's through your teeth," Kerry reminded.

Laura spit and barely missed her target, landing six inches in front of the rock.

"That's it. Now get out of here," Charlie said gruffly.

"One more try! One more try! That will prove it, once and for all."

"That's dirty, Laura. You said only one."

"A second try and I'll never bug you again."

"Do it! Do it! And then get out of here."

"This is it," Laura readied herself. She spit through her teeth and hit high on the side of the rock.

"I did it! I did it!" Laura jumped in the air, shouting happily. "I did it!"

She headed for the church entrance where she saw a friend starting up the stairs.

"I did it, Heidi! I can spit with the boys."

Totally confused, Heidi took a step backwards to avoid Laura's touch.

Charlie and Kerry gave up and walked toward the church.

Kerry paused on the steps and asked Charlie, "Did you read this evening's paper?"

"Not yet, why?"

"There's a short paragraph on page three. It says someone stole a silver candlestick from somebody's house last night. They didn't take anything else—just a candlestick."

"The Captain. The police are going to catch him if we don't do something."

"Worse yet, somebody in a tan hat is going to shoot him climbing through a back window. Who do you think that creep was who followed you into the woods?"

"I'm not sure," Charlie answered. "He might have something to do with the candlesticks. I'm not sure."

"I still think we should tell the police."

"Maybe we should, but I don't want to take any chances on getting Captain Rankin arrested. I still think we can get him out of this."

Charlie and Pete pushed off in their green rowboat and headed out in the Bay. They carried a set of long handled tongs and a bushel basket. Once they had rowed out to a depth of 10 or 20 feet, they would try their skill at tonging oysters.

Tossing the anchor in, they began the hard job of holding the huge tongs. It was awkward for an experienced waterman and extremely difficult for young people.

Charlie pushed the tongs against the bottom and felt something solid. Assuming they were shells he opened the tongs and took a bite. Careful to hold them closed, Charlie pulled straight up and dumped its contents into his basket. Mud, crab shells, a beer can and half a dozen oysters tumbled into the container.

"Neat, man!" Pete pulled a large oyster out with his rubber gloves. "Look how big this jobbie is."

"I'll bet it's one of the old ones. Some of these live to be 10 or 20 years old."

Pete groped in his pocket for his knife. "Let's eat one. I'll split it with you."

"Okay, but wash the mud off first."

Pete swished his catch in the water and then began to pry it open. The shell was stubborn and creaked when it gave way.

"Boy, they're ugly," Pete said, as he sliced it in two. "What could be dumber than an oyster?" Pete daringly gulped the oyster. He handed the other half to Charlie, who, with a grimace, swallowed the slimy flesh.

"They aren't completely dumb," Charlie said as he lowered his tongs a second time. "In fact, they have to make one big decision when they're young. They figure out where to attach themselves and they stay there the rest of their lives—at least until we gather them."

Charlie swung his collection over the basket and dropped it in. Pete sifted through the assortment and threw back everything that wasn't a full oyster.

"When it's little, an oyster settles to the bottom. It uses its foot to find its way around. If it feels mud under it, the oyster moves on until it finds something hard, like a piece of oyster shell."

"How does it hold on to the shell?"

"The foot shoots out some sticky glue. In a few minutes the oyster is stuck for good. Then the foot becomes part of the oyster's body. That's why you don't have to buy shoes for oysters—ha, ha."

Pete threw back part of an old shoe. "Why aren't you supposed to eat oysters caught in months without R's?"

"The biggest reason is that they don't taste as good. Their bodies change in the summer. It isn't dangerous to eat them; they just don't taste as good."

"Where do you learn all this junk?"

"If you would read more you'd learn it too. All you

do is watch monster movies."

Pete smoothed out their 18 oysters in the bottom of the basket. He had washed them off and packed them neatly.

"Are we going to keep going back to that old ship?" Pete asked.

"Why sure. We can't abandon old Captain Rankin. You guys really sound chicken. What are you afraid of—ghosts?"

"I'm not too excited about what might be in that other room, but that isn't all. Kerry told me about the man in the woods."

"That probably has nothing to do with it. He was just some looney."

"But there's also Mom and Dad. They're going to blow their stacks when they find out we're going out there."

"Will you let me handle them? When they find out we're helping someone, they'll understand. They want us to help people."

"Then why don't we tell them now? They could help us to help."

"Sure—they'll call the police. I keep telling you guys, we don't want the Captain arrested."

"I don't feel so good about it. The Bible tells us to *obey* our parents."

"Great! I didn't hear you say that when you smoked the paper bag. I didn't hear you say that when you got kicked out of English class."

"But still, it does say that."

"I'll handle it, Pete. Just trust me."

Chapter Six

Math wasn't Charlie's favorite class and some days he had to struggle to keep from falling asleep. Mr. Taylor's voice sounded like the low hum of a buzz saw. Whenever Charlie was bored, his mind started searching for odd things to do.

Today, he tried all sorts of mental tricks, but none seemed to work. Charlie had counted how many times Mr. Taylor's forehead wrinkled as he spoke. Three times he had counted the ceiling tiles and multiplied them by seven. Nothing was working. Mr. Taylor's droning was sending Charlie into a slumber.

It was too late for Kerry, sitting in front of Charlie. Counting tiles and playing mental Pac-Man had not worked this time. Kerry's head was slumped on his chest in a deep sleep.

In half a second Charlie brightened up. He knew how to make the class come to life.

"Kerry, Kerry," Charlie whispered and shook him briskly. "The teacher called you to the board."

Kerry jerked his head and rubbed his numb face.

"Quick, Kerry," Charlie whispered urgently. "He wants you at the board."

Kerry drowsily forced himself to his feet.

"Go, Kerry, go."

Still half asleep, Kerry tilted and stumbled against the girl sitting to his right. As she glared, everyone looked at the staggering student.

"I've got it," Kerry told Mr. Taylor as he tried to focus through bleary eyes. The teacher stared back in bewilderment.

"I can work the problem."

When Kerry reached the front of the room, he bumped into the teacher's desk, knocking a stack of papers onto the floor. In two more unsteady steps Kerry reached the board and picked up a piece of chalk.

"Now, what's the problem, Mr. Taylor?"

The class had collapsed into uncontrollable laughter. Howls and screams filled the room as the students watched Kerry's confused movements.

A red blush started to flood Kerry's face as he realized what had happened to him.

"Kerry," Mr. Taylor said crisply, "sit down."

As Kerry retreated to his chair, even the teacher began laughing.

Kerry sank low into his chair. "Really cute, Charlie. Really cute!"

Charlie set up his father's camera and tripod on the bank in his backyard and began adjusting the focus.

"I get to take the first picture," Laura insisted.

"Why?"

"Because I paid for the film."

"What is film without a camera?" Charlie moved the tripod three feet closer to the shoreline.

"We take turns, like you said, Charlie. You try to cheat me and I'll throw you into the Bay."

"Don't get so riled up. And cool the threats. You're going to scare the loons away."

"I still get the first shot."

Charlie backed away. "So take it—take it."

Laura could see the birds clearly as they sat on the quiet Bay. They were easy to spot because of the white collar around their black striped necks. Their backs were covered with black and white checks.

"Well, will you take the picture?"

"You don't rush art," Laura said slowly.

"Art? I could *paint* the picture before you take one."

Snap.

"Now let a pro do it."

"It will probably blur. All of your pictures blur."

"Shhh. I'll get him just as he dives. That will be a prize winner—a diving loon."

"While you're waiting, I have a great idea we should consider."

"I wouldn't bet on how great it is, but I'm willing to listen. What's it about?"

"Captain Rankin. I think I've got a great plan to get him off the ship."

"Hold it—hold it."

Snap.

"I think I've got it. A real loon diving for food. Most people never even get to see one, let alone photograph it."

Laura moved to the camera for her turn. She spoke as she swiveled it to the left.

"What if we go out to the ship," she said, "and steal the candlesticks from Captain Rankin? Then we can tell him we'll give them back if he moves to land."

Snap.

"That way we can protect the Captain before someone hurts him or the police arrest him for stealing candlesticks."

Charlie prepared to take his turn. "What if he gets

mad and just shoots us?"

"That nice old man isn't going to shoot a bunch of kids. Besides, we have to find out who is in that other room."

"I thought you didn't want to go out there."

"I don't," Laura explained, "but we're too far into this to give up now. Let's get it over with—quickly—before someone gets hurt."

"You might be making sense."

"Besides that, we might be sitting ducks, or loons, for this nut who followed us into the woods. I don't want him using me for target practice."

"I'll have to think this one over."

"You mean you hate to admit I'm right?"

"It isn't that, though you don't seem to be right very often."

"Go ahead, duck lips. Think it over. Change the plan just a little so you won't have to admit that a 'mere girl' had a good idea."

"Yak, yak, yak. I told you I'd think it over—and it will probably work."

"Well, don't think too long. That galloping ghost in the woods might be looking for Captain Rankin and us too."

After dinner the Dean family agreed to take out some old games and spend the evening together. They finally decided on "Monopoly." Even though it took a long time to play, everyone enjoyed the challenge. To speed up the game they shuffled the property and dealt it out. Half the fun was trying to trade quickly and make a set.

"I'll trade you Vermont for Boardwalk," Charlie offered Pete.

"Straight up?" Pete's voice rose, "You have Park

Place. You'll kill us. Look at the rent for houses and hotels."

"How about if I give you Baltic too?"

"Baltic—you're a regular Santa Claus. With a hotel it's only worth $250 for this one and $450 for that one."

"C'mon. Vermont and Baltic for Boardwalk. Is it a deal?" Charlie held the cards up for Pete to see.

"Plus two free trips if I land on any of your property."

"That's against the rules. You can't give free trips—tell him, Dad."

Mr. Dean picked up the dice. "I'll go ahead and roll while you two settle it."

Pete gave in. "It's a deal. Can I build?"

"When it's your turn, son."

"I don't know why I play this game," Pete grumbled. "Mom always wins it anyway."

"Not every time," she objected. "But, it is fun to see what you can do."

"There are too many rules for me," Pete complained. "Go here. Do that. Go to jail. Pay this. It's too much like school."

Charlie said, "If there were no rules we would never get the game played. You could refuse to roll or to pay rent or do anything." He put a hotel on Boardwalk and another one on Park Place. "It's hard enough to get you to move as it is. That's a cool 2,000 bucks if you land here and 1,500 for Park Place."

Pete grabbed the dice. "I didn't think you were too great at keeping rules." He rolled. "I could say a few things about you and rules—but I won't."

"One, two, three, four, five," Charlie counted happily as he moved Pete's man. "That'll be $2,000. I ought to charge you another $200 for talking so much."

"I don't know what's going on," said Mrs. Dean, "but you two sound a little irritated about something."

"Before we take the candlesticks, we have to find out what is in that other room," Charlie explained as Kerry rowed the boat in the evening twilight. "You two will have to keep Captain Rankin busy while Laura and I rescue whoever is doing all that screaming. Give me some more shoe polish."

Laura and Charlie were smearing black polish on their faces and hands. Each was dressed in a dark jacket and trousers.

"What about that musket?" Pete asked. "If he hears you sneaking around he'll start shooting that thing."

"I've thought about that," Charlie said calmly. "In the first place, Laura and I won't make a sound. In the second place, I don't think that gun is loaded."

"You don't think it's loaded?" Kerry said in a shrill voice. "We're the ones he'll be pointing it at."

"Don't worry about it. I've thought it all through."

"Including our funerals?" Pete quipped.

"Remember," said Charlie, as he tied the boat to the ladder on the freighter, "we'll give you exactly five minutes to get Captain Rankin out of the room and to the bow. We'll then have ten minutes to get in, rescue the man, or whatever, and get him to the boat. Then we'll go back after the candlesticks. That'll take another ten minutes. Pete, check your watch with Laura's."

"Twenty minutes after you've taken Captain Rankin outside, you'll make an excuse and join us in the boat."

Kerry started for the ladder. "I don't like this at all."

"It'll work beautifully." Charlie assured. "They did something like this on television once." He reached for the stretcher.

"On television!" Kerry whispered loudly. "You got this scheme from some goofy TV show?"

Charlie pushed him up. "Don't worry. I changed it around to fit us."

Kerry and Pete hurried up the ladder while Charlie and Laura waited. The stretcher they held was made of canvas and two wooden boards. Charlie's father had bought it cheap at a secondhand store.

"Captain Rankin, have you seen the osprey that's making its nest on the ship?" Kerry asked him nervously. "Come on outside and we'll show you."

The Captain laughed and followed the two boys toward the bow. At precisely the five-minute mark, Charlie and Laura stepped lightly onto the shadowy ship and headed for the mysterious room.

"There are a lot more ospreys around the Bay than there used to be," Pete said. "Don't you think so?"

Charlie whispered to Laura, "On three, I'll throw open the door. I'll crawl in and you stand up straight. That way they won't know there are two of us."

"Why don't *you* stand up and *I'll* crawl in?"

"Yours is not to reason why. Yours is but to do or die."

"Baloney."

Charlie threw open the door and dove for the floor

with the stretcher in one hand. With eyes wide as pizzas, Laura stiffly walked in.

The room was quiet and dark as a cave. Charlie felt around him as he inched across the floor. Laura ran her hands along the wall very carefully.

"Better go back inside now. Hee, Hee, Hee!" Captain Rankin, musket in hand, began walking away.

"Wait a minute," Kerry called. "Don't you want to see if there's a nest on the starboard side? I've never seen an osprey nest before."

Pete looked at his watch and held up five fingers three times.

Captain Rankin pointed the musket at Kerry's stomach. "Are you guys up to something funny?"

"Oh, no. We just want to see the nest."

"Okay. Hee, Hee, Hee!" The captain smiled. "Let's give it a look."

Laura's hands continued to feel their way along the wall until they found a shelf. Her fingers slid lightly along, ready to fly if they touched anything scary. Soon she felt something furry and soft. Laura cautiously felt the outline of a small animal.

"Whatever it is, Lord, let it be dead," she whispered.

Slowly, her fingers crept on. They moved across what felt like a nose and then touched something cold like an eye. She swallowed hard. Laura moved her hands and decided to search somewhere else.

"Here, over here," Charlie called. "I think I've found him. Laura followed the sound of his voice.

"He's stiff—he might be dead. Feel his face."

"No thanks."

"Let's roll him onto the stretcher."

"He's not very heavy."

"Must have lost a lot of weight," said Charlie, and he lifted the man's shoulders onto the stretcher. "It feels like he's wearing a uniform. He must be a soldier or something."

"Let's strap him down."

Captain Rankin again began to walk away. "Well, that's enough ospreys. Hee, Hee, Hee! We'd better go inside."

Pete held up five fingers for Kerry to see. "Oops!" Kerry shouted and stumbled over his own feet. He hit the deck with a loud thud and sprawled out.

"My ankle, my ankle."

Captain Rankin and Pete quickly crouched by his side.

"I twisted my ankle, terrible."

"Wait here, I'll get some ice."

"Oh, no!" Pete interrupted. "I think we could just massage his ankle and he'll be better in no time."

Without objecting, the Captain began to vigorously rub the fallen boy's limb.

"You take the front end," Charlie commanded in a loud whisper.

They started toward the door, carrying the stretcher, with Laura in the lead.

WHAM! They struck the wall, nearly knocking the stretcher out of their hands.

"Slow down, Charlie!"

"Shhh."

They moved out of the room and hustled toward the ladder.

"See if you guys can help me up," Kerry said to Pete and Captain Rankin. He wrapped his arms over their shoulders. They had to struggle to lift him off the deck.

Leaning heavily toward Captain Rankin, Kerry forced the elderly man to lean backwards. As the man lost his footing, all three tumbled across the deck, sending arms and legs flying in every direction. Captain Rankin accidentally dropped his musket.

"Get off, get off," Captain Rankin grunted. "You boys are worse than a dizzy tightrope walker."

In one swift move he collected his musket and pointed it at Kerry and Pete.

"Don't push so hard," Laura demanded in a husky whisper as they reached the side of the ship. She rested her end of the stretcher on the metal railing as she climbed onto the ladder.

As Laura started down, Charlie edged the stretcher over to her.

"Do you have it?" he asked.

"You bet."

"Can you hold him?"

"Don't worry."

"I'm going to let go while I climb over. Are you sure you can handle it?"

"Stop talking and let's go."

"Okay, it's all yours. I'm climbing over."

Charlie swung his leg over the side.

"Hold on. I'm coming."

"I'm okay. Don't you—oh, oh, oh. . . . ."

SPLASH!

Charlie's jaw dropped as he heard something crash into the Bay.

"I dropped him!" Laura shouted.

Charlie and Laura scrambled down the ladder and dove into the water.

"Turn him over!" Charlie yelled as they reached the stretcher floating face-down in the water.

With a strong push they righted the stretcher, then dog-paddled to the boat pulling the stretcher behind. Awkwardly, they pushed the victim aboard and pulled themselves up. Charlie and Laura sat in the moonlight gasping for breath.

"We had better check this guy's windpipe," Laura suggested. "We may have drowned the poor fellow."

The victim's eyes were wide open in a horrible stare. Charlie and Laura looked at each other despondently. They saw no sign of breathing.

"We're probably too late." Charlie reached inside the soldier's coat to feel for a heartbeat.

Laura tried to open his mouth and check his breathing.

"What's this?" she asked in dismay. "This is no person. His head is rubber."

Charlie's shoulders drooped. "It's a rubber mannequin. We did all of that to rescue a mannequin."

"Now look what a mess you got us into, Mr. Wise Guy."

"Sure. And who knows what kind of trouble Kerry and Pete are in."

Chapter Seven

Charlie and Laura hurried up the ladder. When they reached the deck, they paused for a few moments.

"I'll bet we've taken twenty minutes with this," Charlie thought aloud.

"I wonder where they are?"

"We'd better act quickly. If Captain Rankin finds his dummy missing, we might be in bad shape."

"Let's check the bow first."

As they hurried forward, they heard someone running in their direction. Quickly they stepped back into a doorway. Someone raced past in the darkness.

"I think that was Kerry," Laura said.

"Shhh!"

A second person ran by.

"That was Captain Rankin chasing Kerry."

"Hold on there, you little pirate!" the Captain shouted.

A third person soon followed. Charlie leaped out to grab Pete. Pete jumped with fright.

"It's us, Pete."

"Where have you two been? That old coot is trying to shoot us."

"We've had some problems. And we haven't gotten the candlesticks yet."

"Forget the candlesticks," said Pete, shaking.

"This Rankin guy is cr-a-a-a-zy!"

"You can handle it, Pete. We need five more minutes to get those candlesticks. You two can outrun him for that long."

"Sure you can," Laura added.

"What about that musket?"

Charlie patted Pete on the shoulder. "I'll bet he isn't even a good shot."

"Yeah, you'll bet my neck on it."

"Five minutes, Pete," Charlie demanded. "It means everything. Watch out."

They ducked back into the doorway as Kerry ran past again. Captain Rankin followed. He seemed to be losing ground.

"All right, Charlie, but this is the last favor."

Pete jumped out onto the deck.

"Captain Rankin!" he yelled. "You forgot about *me*!"

The old man stopped and paused as if he couldn't decide whom to chase. After two shakes of his head, the Captain went after Pete, with his musket waving high above his head.

"Come back here, you fat-bellied vulture!"

Laura pulled at Charlie's arm. "We'd better get at it."

They ran to Captain Rankin's room and opened the door. A gas lantern gave off a spooky light. It was exactly the way they remembered it—the huge balls of twine, the bushel baskets full of crabs' claws, the one-stringed guitar against the wall. On the shelf they spotted the eight beautiful silver candlesticks.

"Find a bag—something to carry these things in," said Charlie.

Laura held up a tote bag. "Let's use this." On its

side was a picture of the lighthouse at Thomas Island.

They packed seven of the candlesticks into the bag, but the eighth wouldn't fit. Laura held it while Charlie carried the bag.

"Come back here, you two sea snakes!"

Charlie and Laura could hear Captain Rankin shouting as they arrived on the top deck.

"Let's secure the candlesticks first," Charlie suggested. "Then we'll find a way to help Kerry and Pete."

They dashed down the ladder and placed their cargo safely in the boat. Without a word, they pivoted and raced back up to the deck.

"Here they come!" Laura called out.

Captain Rankin was winded and slow, but he kept running. Kerry was coming up behind the old man.

"Over here!" Charlie shouted. "Over here!"

The Captain stopped, looked in several directions and then started after Charlie.

"No!" Laura said excitedly. "I'm over here!"

Totally confused, the Captain stopped again and then ran for Laura. They both disappeared on the other side of the ship.

"Come here, Pete!" Charlie cried as he motioned. "Kerry, we have to put our heads together!"

Pete glanced around. "We'll probably have to trip him or something so we can get out of here."

Kerry said, gasping, "When he finds out the candleholders are gone, he's liable to start shooting that old cannon of his."

"I think I have an idea," Charlie said slowly as he thought. "Watch out, here they come."

"That guy can run forever," Pete said. "He's slowing down, but he's far from finished."

Charlie ordered, "All of you head for the side and wait for me." He leaped out in front of Captain Rankin. "I took your candlesticks!" he yelled as he took Laura's place.

Laura turned off to the side as Captain Rankin went after Charlie. The Captain kept steadily after him, but was beginning to develop a hobble.

Kerry, Pete and Laura climbed over the side and rattled down the rusted ladder. Once safely in the boat, they untied the rope and Kerry took the oars. He kept the boat close to the ship.

"Come on, Charlie," Laura whispered anxiously, "we're ready to go."

"What's this?" Pete asked.

"It's the man we rescued," Laura admitted shyly.

"You rescued a rubber mannequin? It won't get you the Red Cross award for bravery."

Kerry started to laugh. "Maybe you'll win the rubber duck award."

Laura looked up at the ladder. "Will you two cool it? Charlie could be getting himself killed while you're joking around."

Charlie continued his jog around the ship, making sure he stayed a safe distance ahead of the Captain. As he ran, Charlie tried to think of a way to dash for the ladder without getting shot.

Suddenly he stopped next to a wall and pulled off his wet tee shirt. Captain Rankin came around the corner and got a glimpse of Charlie standing there.

"Hold still, you thief, or I'll part your hair between your eyes."

Without hesitating, Charlie threw his white shirt over Captain Rankin's head, and spun the old man around. The Captain called Charlie a long list of sea curses as he continued to whirl.

Charlie let go of his angry victim and made a mad leap for the side. Missing half the steps on the way down, Charlie jumped from the ladder to the waiting boat.

"Row as fast as you can," Charlie ordered.

As they pulled out across the Bay, Captain Rankin appeared at the railing.

"Come back, you lizards! You yellow-bellied toads. I'll hang you all from the ship's mast. Come back, you pirates!"

Four exhausted young people slumped in the rowboat. Kerry slowly pumped the oars. Laura's hair hung across her forehead and flopped down her neck in wet lumps. The night breeze was cold.

Charlie was without his jacket and his shirt. Sitting stiffly, he didn't want to admit he was freezing.

Pete broke the silence. "A cool job, Charlie. I mean, the terrific way you two saved this poor rubber dummy. Who else could have done it? He probably has a rubber wife and two little rubber kids in a store window who have been worried sick about him. They're going to be so grateful."

Charlie didn't answer. He shot a cold, icy look into the eyes of his younger brother. His grimace looked like he could bite a piece out of steel.

"All right, all right." Pete turned away to look out into the darkness. "Man, no sense of humor."

The next day, they met after basketball practice at Andy's Drive-In. It was a favorite place for young people around Collins Landing. The drive-in served great pizza by the slice, burgers, floats, soda, onion rings and plenty of french fries. Oyster sandwiches and crab cakes were two of their main features. If you sat anywhere near the kitchen, your mouth would water from the strong seafood aroma.

"Where are we now?" Kerry asked with concern as he opened the wrappings on his hot dogs. He squeezed mounds of mustard on the chopped onions.

"We are in Andy's," Laura answered, sipping her soda.

"That's not what I meant," Kerry said with his mouth full. "I meant about this candlestick thing. The way I see it, we haven't accomplished a thing."

Pete was dumping ketchup on his fries. "How do you figure?"

"Well, so far we've been chased around a ship, stolen some stolen candleholders—" Kerry paused for a drink—"and we've had some sawdust brain shoot at us. For what?"

Charlie picked at his crab cake. "Actually, we're in great shape. Can you believe we actually got the candlesticks? Now all we have to do is get Captain Rankin to come ashore. The police will go easy on him and we'll have stopped a crime. Talk about great minds."

"Sure," Pete spoke up, "and when it's over, Mom and Dad will know we were on that crummy ship. Then are we going to hear about it."

"Big deal. They won't say a thing. When they hear how smoothly we pulled this off, they'll probably buy us new bikes," Charlie reasoned.

"Besides, you worry too much," Laura added. "If worry made your ears grow, you'd look like Dumbo."

"Really cute," Pete said, and reached into his

jeans pocket. "Girls always have to get lippy." He whipped out his pocketknife, flipped it open, and poked a hole in Laura's soda cup, pouring its contents onto the table.

Laura quickly put her finger on the small hole. "You're a mean kid!"

"Don't worry about it," Pete said with a smile, " 'cuz your ears might start growing."

Charlie finished his crab cake. "I've got the plan worked out. I know how to get Captain Rankin ashore and I can arrange a peaceful meeting with the police. The only thing is, we'll have to take another trip out to the ship."

"Forget it," Pete blurted.

"My mother would never let me go," Kerry said.

"Come on," Laura teased. "You two tough guys can't chicken out now. Besides, we can't drop Captain Rankin right in the middle of this. The sooner we go, the better."

They left Andy's and headed for the pier. As they walked down the street, they continued to argue over what to try next. The group turned left at the first corner.

"Laura, do you have any paper on you?" Charlie asked. "Kerry, get some stones—about quarter size. We can wrap notes around stones. Laura, I asked, 'Do you have any paper on you?' "

Charlie stopped.

"Laura. Where's Laura?"

"She was right behind me," said Kerry as he looked around.

"Maybe she went into a store."

"Laura! Laura!" Charlie called. "Where are you?"

"Girls," Pete chirped. "They never tell you anything."

"I hope she stopped in a store," Charlie said. "But I'm not so sure."

"Be quiet, girl, keep your hands up." The man in the tan hat stood behind Laura and held his hand tightly over her mouth. "You make any noise and you'll be sorry."

He let go of Laura and reached quickly inside his coat to draw out his revolver. She turned to face the tall man with the scar on his face.

"You and your friends know where those candlesticks are, and I'm not fooling around. You tell me where; I'll go get them and leave you alone."

"Who are you?" Laura asked breathlessly.

"What do you care? I've got a gun."

"How do I know you'll let me go?"

"I always let people go. They give me their money, or whatever, and I always let them go."

"That's what *you* say. But after I tell you, you might shoot me."

"Don't you trust me?"

"Of course not. You're a crook."

"That doesn't mean you can't trust me. You really know how to hurt someone's feelings."

"Well, don't pout. Maybe you are an honest crook."

"Sure," he said with a smile.

"Why don't you give me your name on a piece of paper."

"You think I'm crazy? Then you would know who I am."

"It isn't that. It's just that if I put your name in my pocket, I know you won't shoot me—because when the police find my body, they'll find your name in my pocket. Doesn't that make sense?"

"I never thought of it that way."

"If you expect someone to trust a crook, you have to be fair."

"All right. But I'm still not too crazy about the idea. Do you have a piece of paper?"

"I think so. You don't mind if I lower my hands do you?"

"'Course not."

"Here," Laura handed him a piece of paper, and a pencil she had saved from a miniature golf game.

"Hold this, will you?" The man extended his gun toward Laura. "Never mind." He drew it back. "You don't think I'd do something dumb like that, do you?" He tucked the gun under his arm. "Turn around, will you, so I can write on your back."

When he was finished, he handed the note to Laura.

"Butch Wanek," she read aloud and then slipped it into her pocket.

"Now, enough of this stalling." He pointed the gun at Laura. "I want to know where those candlesticks are—now."

"And tell me again what happens if I don't tell you."

"You know what will happen." The crook stuck his gun close to her face.

"Okay, okay. I'll tell you, but listen carefully. You go down this street to the corner, and you take a left, another left, a right, another left, a right, a left, two rights and go straight for one block."

"Wait a minute. A left, a right, another left, a right, another right—"

"No, no. You take a left, another left, a right, a

left, two rights, and go straight for two blocks."

"I thought you said one block," he corrected.

"That's right. You're too smart to be a crook."

"I guess so," he mumbled, and blushed. "One more time—I take a left."

"Right."

"A right?"

"No, a left."

"A left?"

"Right."

"A right?"

"No, a left."

"A left?"

"Right."

"A right?"

"No, a left."

"A left?"

"Right."

"A right?"

"No, a left."

"A left?"

"Right."

"A right?"

"Look, it might be better if I took you there."

"Okay."

Laura led with Butch close behind. He kept his hand on the revolver in his pocket. As Laura began turning corners, she looked in each direction for her friends. Maybe a policeman would come along—anyone to get her out of this mess.

"Don't we take a left here?" Butch asked.

"Right."

"Not left?"

"Yes."

"Left."

"Right."

"I think I'll just follow you."

Laura's eyes moved rapidly looking for some way to escape her captor. After walking for about ten tense minutes, she saw Charlie as she glanced out of the corner of her eye. He, Kerry and Pete were following and getting closer.

"I think this is it," Laura pointed to a large, green dumpster next to a group of apartment buildings. "We hid it in the bottom. It's a brown sack."

Laura stepped up on a cinder block and reached in. "I can't see it yet, but I know it's here."

"Move, kid. I'll find it."

He stood on the block and bent over, riffling through the trash.

"Are you sure it's here?" his voice echoed.

"Keep digging."

When Charlie, Kerry and Pete arrived, Laura silently pointed at the man. Smoothly all four walked up behind him and pushed.

"Hey, what is this?" He yelled as he sprawled head first into the trash. "Let me out of here!"

Chapter Eight

"Don't throw stones," Charlie warned as he grabbed Kerry's arm. "Watch what that duck is doing."

"I'll bet I can hit it."

"No. Be still."

The duck dropped its head under the water and came up wiggling its neck.

"It's eating clams," Charlie explained.

"How does it get them out of the shells?"

"It doesn't. The small clams are just swallowed whole."

"A duck can eat a whole clam, shell and all?"

"They've got tough stomachs. They just grind up the shells inside and eat the clams."

"Wouldn't it be great if we could do that? We could just swallow a can of sardines and later just spit out the can. Now, that's tough."

"Come on, we've got to get to school. You stick with me on today's field trip and I'll teach you lots." Charlie retrieved his lunch bag from a nearby picnic table and walked away.

If Charlie rode across the Bay Bridge a million times, he would probably never be bored. The height of the bridge, the sea gulls pumping across the sky, the ships and yachts cutting through the chopping waves never ceased to fascinate him.

Baltimore was a great city to visit, but Charlie would never want to live there—too many people and cars and not enough fish, crabs, eels and clams. The Orioles were a great baseball team, but were not enough reason for him to live in a big city. Even the Colts couldn't keep him from the Bay.

The new National Aquarium was the main goal of their field trip, but there was plenty more to see around Inner Harbor.

Kerry stared up at the glass ceiling of the Aquarium. "I'll bet this place cost a billion bucks. All this fancy architecture. Maybe two billion bucks."

"Sharks and rays," Charlie marveled. "I've never seen a ray this close. If you see one in the Bay, it's usually too dark to make it out well."

Laura walked away. "I don't want to see one in the Bay."

"Look how long these eels are." Charlie was enthused.

"Let's not," Laura insisted.

"Boy, you're grouchy today," Kerry said as he made faces at the fish.

"Let's take her upstairs and feed her to the piranhas," Charlie suggested.

"Are there piranhas in the Bay?" Kerry wondered.

"No, dense. There are more things here than just fish from the Bay."

At nearby Pier 4, the class toured a World War II submarine. Sharp, pointed teeth were painted across the dark gray bow, making it look like a steel sea monster.

"This is spooky," said Kerry as they climbed down the metal stairs inside the submarine.

"It all looks so small," Laura observed.

"I love it. I love it, I tell you." Charlie stretched his

arms out when he reached the bottom. "I've got to be a submarine captain. Not on one of these old jobs, but on a new nuclear one. 'Drop periscope. Prepare to dive.' "

"Look how neat and clean it is," Laura said.

"They always keep them this way," Charlie said with authority. "They scrub them night and day. Not me, of course; I'll be the captain. I'll just sit and tell my crew when to fire the torpedoes."

"We ought to have this to take us out to see Rankin next time," Kerry suggested. "We could just pop up out of the water and demand he surrender. Then we could whisk him away to safety."

"I tell you, I'm not going out there again," Kerry objected as he stood by the rowboat.

"We have to," Charlie argued. "Captain Rankin has no idea where the candlesticks are and we have to give him a clue before he does something foolish."

"I'll go out there with you guys, but I'm not going up on the ship." Laura stepped into the boat. "He'll be so mad this time, he'll shoot someone for sure."

"Don't be so chicken." Charlie carried a cardboard box under his arm. "I've got the plan and the capability right here. Captain Rankin will get the message."

They each found a spot in the boat and pushed off. The sun was disappearing beyond the horizon, but they were used to cool evening trips.

"Why do I always have to row?" Kerry muttered.

As they pulled alongside the freighter, Charlie began to whisper orders.

"Pete, hand out the slingshots. This way none of us has to take any chances."

They were wide wooden slings with thick red

rubber bands. It took some extra strength to pull them back.

"Notes are tied around the stones. We can just shoot them up on the deck. Then no one will get hurt."

"What do they say?" Laura placed a note into her sling.

"Don't point it at anybody," Charlie warned. "They have enough power to kill an animal at fifty yards. It tells Captain Rankin to be at Woody's General Store at 7:00 on Tuesday night. Once he gets that far, we can figure out a way to get him to the police."

"Aren't these a lot of notes?" Kerry asked.

"I thought about that, but we can't take any chances of him not finding at least one note on the deck," Charlie explained.

Laura aimed at the sky. "There must be fifty of them."

"That's about twelve apiece. Let's get started." Charlie loaded his slingshot and pointed it up the side of the ship.

"Ready. Aim. Fire!"

Four paper wads burst into the air. Two notes cleared the side and the other two dropped into the Bay.

"Again."

Four more missiles rocketed up and over the side.

"That's better." Charlie grabbed another one. "This won't take long."

Whap! Whap! The assault continued.

"Hey, what's that?" Laura shouted.

CLANK! A rusty chain crashed against the side of the boat.

"He's attacking us!" Kerry yelled.

"Look out!" Pete pointed up as an old bucket

came tumbling through the air.

"Let's run for it." Charlie pushed away from the side of the ship. Kerry took one oar while Laura grabbed the other.

"Watch it!" Charlie shouted.

A heavy fish net plummeted over Pete's head, entangling his arms.

"Row, guys, row!" Charlie ordered as he covered his head with his arms.

Thump!

A bag of oyster shells smashed across the bow of the boat.

"Faster, faster!" Charlie urged.

As they pulled away from the ship, objects continued to be hurled in their direction—a large arch handled spoon; a hammer; a long, black board; an old crab pot; a broken oar.

With each missile, Captain Rankin called them names and jumped up and down with frustration. Far from the ship, they could still see his fist shaking in the air.

The next day after school, Kerry came over to Charlie's yard. Charlie was busy repairing the wiring on some of his crab pots.

Kerry picked up a piece of wire and handed it to Charlie, and said, "I don't know if I can make it tonight."

"Don't tell me you're going to chicken out?"

"It isn't that. There's just no way to know what that crazy old captain is going to do. He might come into Woody's firing guns—or swinging a sword like a dizzy pirate. I tell you, that man isn't normal."

"You don't think Chesapeake Charlie is going to

let you down, do you?" He gave his pliers a couple of firm twists. "I've got it all planned out."

Kerry sat down on the bench. "I don't know. I want to help, but I'm not too anxious to get killed."

"It won't happen. I've got it all figured out." Charlie joined him on the bench.

Kerry held up a green and red paper pouch. "Look what I brought from my uncle."

"Your uncle gave you *that*?"

"I didn't say he gave it to me—but he wouldn't mind me taking it. He likes me to try new things."

"Not chewing tobacco, Kerry. Anything but chewing tobacco."

"You don't have to try any." Kerry pulled out some tobacco between his fingers and thumb. He packed it into the side of his mouth. A small lump puffed up on his cheek.

"How does it taste?"

"Not bad. You see those football players and cowboys on television chew it all the time."

"Hey, don't spit it on the ground. My parents will find the stuff."

"Okay. It's just as easy to swallow the juice."

"Swallow it?" Charlie looked pained.

"It isn't that bad. In fact, it's sort of tasty."

"If you're afraid to try it, that's all right." Kerry gave the wad an occasional chew, like gum. "Everybody's chicken sometimes."

"It's not that. It's—it's—well—okay, but just a *little* pinch."

"Sure, help yourself."

Hesitantly, Charlie took out a pinch. It was only half as much as Kerry took, but it looked big to Charlie.

Charlie wrinkled his nose. "It smells strong."

"You'll get used to it."

"It'd be nice if you could spit."

"Yeah, but what do people do who chew it in the house? They can't spit. I'm getting used to it."

"Me too."

Kerry rubbed his forehead. "I didn't realize how tired I was until I sat down."

"Here comes Laura," Charlie nodded. "Let's not tell her. She'll just make fun of us."

Laura spoke as she approached the bench. "I think I have a great idea about how to handle tonight."

"What is it?" Charlie asked, trying to keep his lips as tight as possible.

"What's wrong with you?" asked Laura.

"What do you mean?"

"When you talk, something brown runs down the side of your mouth."

"Oh, that's nothing."

"Yeah," Kerry quipped, "his tongue is just rotting."

"You, too. You both have brown junk caked around your lips."

"It's a boy thing," Charlie said.

"Another boy thing—just like that spitting contest I won. I can do *any* boy thing."

"Not this one," Kerry challenged.

Laura put her hands on her hips. "Anything, guys, anything."

Charlie said, "I dare you." His eyes were beginning to droop.

"Anything, guys."

Kerry held up the package. "It's chewing tobacco."

"Well, I didn't mean *that*."

Charlie swallowed again. "You said 'anything.' And anything means anything."

"Okay. I'm no chicken." Laura sat down next to Kerry. "Give me some."

Kerry handed her the pouch and she took out a pinch. Reluctantly, Laura stuffed it in her mouth.

"There's only one catch," Charlie said. "You can't spit it out—can't get it on the grass."

"It's all right with me." Laura's voice lacked the confidence it had earlier.

"I'm not feeling all that great," Kerry admitted.

"Tell me this. Did anybody see that tree move?" Charlie asked dryly. "I'm not feeling all that great either."

"You guys lose again. Actually, I rather like the stuff. Let's face it, boys are definitely an inferior race. I'll bet you, given time, girls can do anything boys can do. It feels great to be a girl."

"Cool it, Chatter Jaws," Kerry told her, "the tobacco is making me sick enough. Where can I spit this stuff out?"

"Great idea." Charlie agreed. "Let me get that blue bucket."

"The bucket is *green*, Charlie," Laura said with a laugh. "It's green. Besides, I doubt you can pick it up."

Kerry turned and threw up behind the bench. "Don't bother getting it for me," he choked. He threw up again.

"Ha, ha ha!" Laura forced a cruel laugh. "Girls 2; Boys 0. You guys ought to give up."

Charlie took two steps toward the bucket, but was too dizzy to keep going. He fell to his knees and threw up on the front of his pants.

Laura didn't bother to laugh at Charlie as he fell. She didn't feel as lively as she had a minute before. Her eyes began to close. The backyard seemed to swim a little. She could hear her stomach starting to complain.

"Maybe I should get that bucket," she said to no one in particular.

Laura stood, but her legs did not seem happy about it. Carefully, she coaxed her right leg forward.

"Hee, Hee, Hee! You lousy pirates. I've got you this time."

The terrible laugh ricocheted inside Charlie's slumped head.

"It's Captain Rankin!" Laura screamed.

"I'll chop your heads off, you low-bellied snakes."

Kerry could barely see the fuzzy figure. He struggled to his feet and began running away in an unsteady line.

"I've got you now. Hee, Hee, Hee!"

Confused and nauseated, Laura ran west and started climbing up the back of the Deans' dark blue car. Unsure of what she was on, Laura hoped it led away from the Captain.

Charlie's legs didn't want to cooperate. When he stood up, his stomach revolted again. He couldn't see the Captain at all, but knew where the voice had come from. He took about ten slow steps and then stumbled on a wooden saw-horse. Charlie struggled to regain his footing, but couldn't make his legs move together.

"I'll hang you all, one by one. Hee, Hee, Hee!"

Meanwhile, Kerry had built up a small head of steam and was running at a slow jog. Without knowing it, he ran up onto the wooden pier and headed toward the end. At a steady trot, Kerry ran off the pier and splashed into the Bay.

"Come back! It's me! I was only kidding!" Pete shouted.

Mr. Dean handed Charlie a cup of steaming tea.

"Thanks." Charlie pulled an old blanket around his shoulders. He wasn't sure he could make it to his feet.

"You looked like you needed it. Take your time. Your mother took Kerry and Laura home. It was all we could do to talk her into getting off the car roof." Mr. Dean chuckled. "I thought we might have to drive her home that way."

"The tea tastes good."

Mr. Dean sat down next to Charlie. "I don't suppose you want to try and explain this?"

"Not really. It would be pretty hard. I'm not sure I understand it all."

"Pete didn't say much either. He said he pulled a trick on you and you started running in all directions."

"Pete did it? That was Pete?"

"I believe so, whatever he did."

"Remind me to strangle him."

"Well, I think I understand one thing." Mr. Dean held up the tobacco pouch.

Charlie shivered. "I don't even want to look at it."

"Maybe you want to tell me where you've been going for so many evenings. I have a feeling there's something I ought to know."

"It's not that big a deal, Dad. Besides, it's almost finished. It's just something us guys have been doing. It's okay."

"I hope so. You're usually a good fellow, but sometimes you go pretty far out."

"There are so many things to do, Dad, so many things to try. I love the adventure.

"The way I see it, I'm like one of those striped bass. Most of them are happy to swim around the Bay, but a few have to see more of the world. That's why they head for the ocean. They want to run up and down the Atlantic and see everything. Dad, I can't lead a dull life."

"I understand, Charlie. But don't forget, those bass stay at home for a couple of years first. They learn to swim the Bay before they tackle the Atlantic."

"But most of them never try the ocean. They always play it safe. I've got to try, to find out for myself."

"Sure you do, but first you need to learn some things from your parents. First, you stay inside the boundaries your parents set, then you learn how far you want to go."

"I do listen to you, Dad; that is—most of the time."

"I know you do, Charlie. You are certainly better than most. But, let's aim for *all* the time. 'Children, obey your parents' still makes a lot of sense until you're old enough to decide for yourself. You don't need a big lecture, just a reminder. But remember, don't go outside those boundaries."

Charlie silently nodded his head. Mr. Dean stood to go in.

"Aren't you going to get me in trouble for the chewing tobacco?"

"Not this time. I think the tobacco has been a

better teacher than I could ever be. I've got to go. There's a church board meeting tonight."

"Okay if I go to Woody's after supper? Just good ol' Woody's."

"All right, but maybe your first stop should be the shower."

"You got it."

Charlie staggered to his feet and swayed from side to side.

"You sure you're okay?"

Charlie lifted two fingers to give the victory sign. Then he threw up.

Chapter Nine

"We don't need to call the police yet," Charlie said as they cut through the forest to Woody's store.

"We're taking too many chances," Laura insisted.

"And what if he sees a police car and gets scared away? The best thing we can do is talk him into giving up. Trust me, I can do it." Charlie's legs still felt weak.

Kerry and Pete walked behind. Their thoughts seemed more centered on the Baltimore Colts than on Captain Rankin and cops and robbers.

"I say we all go inside of Woody's, then sit and wait. When Captain Rankin comes in, we'll play it cool and reason with him."

"How well do you think he can reason?" Laura asked. "The last time I saw you talking to the Captain, you threw a damp tee shirt over his head. Now, I'd call that natural charm."

"Did anyone ever tell you you're lippy?"

"All I know is that I'm right."

"Let's cut through the supermarket for a candy bar." Charlie headed inside.

Moving briskly they circled around and headed for the exit near the cash register.

Laura grabbed Charlie's arm, "Look! It's the man in the tan hat."

The man was walking toward them with his hand stuck inside his coat pocket.

"Be careful, he's got that gun," said Charlie. He turned around and collided with Kerry and Pete. "It's the tan hat. This way!"

Walking quickly down the aisle, they lost sight of him.

"Head for the entrance," Charlie commanded.

"Oops!" Pete stopped short. The man was standing at the far end of the aisle. They turned again. With a sharp right they found themselves in the bakery.

The man in the tan hat had hurried around and was coming straight at them. As Charlie, Laura and Kerry turned to get away, Pete picked up a peach pie and hurled it. It splattered on the man's shoulder, but did little to slow him down. Two shoppers saw the pie hit him and screamed in shock.

Their pace increased to a slow run. When Pete reached the frozen food section, he turned left and saw a solid wall of freezers before him. He pivoted to find himself trapped by the man in the tan hat.

"Hold it, kid. I gotta talk to you." He reached out to grab Pete.

Swat! Swat! Two tomatoes crashed against the back of the man's head. The man turned to face his attackers as they ran up the aisle. Pete skirted around him and raced in the other direction. The man started after the other three, but soon lost them.

"Let's get out of here," Kerry whispered to Charlie.

"We can't. Where's Pete? And now we've lost Laura."

Charlie and Kerry hurried down the aisle. A train of shopping carts blocked their escape. They ran back to the other end.

Laura frantically looked for Pete, but was startled to see the man standing in her aisle. Swiftly she pulled two cans of peas from the shelf and rolled one down the aisle toward the running man. Deftly, he stepped aside. The second followed, then a can of lima beans and two cans of corn. Rapid footwork kept him from falling as the volley of ammunition continued to roll.

A lady shopper turned the corner and screamed at the strange battle.

Cans of peaches, baked beans, spinach and pumpkin were rumbling like bowling balls. Laura rolled giant cans of grapefruit juice at her pursuer.

Applesauce finally got him. Failing to lift his right foot high enough, he went tumbling on his face. Laura dashed out of sight.

"Pete, Pete!" Laura half-whispered.

"Where are you?" she heard Charlie call.

Shoppers and clerks gathered to figure out what was going on. They huddled and pointed at the kids.

The man in the tan hat recovered and started back to the bakery section. Stepping cautiously, he tiptoed toward the next aisle. As he gingerly walked next to a gigantic white cooler, he stretched his arms out ready to tackle any of the kids that came into his reach.

Ploof!

A large, fluffy, wedding cake smashed down on his tan hat. Stunned, he stood in a daze while Pete climbed down and ran away. The man shook his head, throwing bits of cake and icing in all directions.

Still bewildered, he took several steps forward and tumbled into a lady shopper. Both of them sprawled on the floor, struggling to gain their footing.

As he started to get up, the man saw a shiny shoe which led to a blue pants leg. Looking up, he saw a huge policeman standing over him with his hands on his hips.

Charlie, Laura, Kerry and Pete barreled out the doors and continued their hectic trip to Woody's. They laughed as they recounted their scary adventure in the supermarket.

"After we settle this thing with the Captain, we can go over to the police and tell them all about the man in the tan hat." Charlie set a rapid pace.

"They won't be very likely to let him go for a while," Laura agreed. "That guy is really creepy."

"And he's not too bright."

"Hurry, it's already past seven. Captain Rankin might get anxious and not wait for us," Charlie warned.

Inside Woody's, Charlie put his plan into action.

"Now, don't forget," he said in low tones, "Laura and I will sit here playing checkers while you two sit off to the side by the potato sacks."

"Then what?" Kerry asked.

"When the Captain comes in, you two circle behind him."

"What if he starts shooting?" Pete wondered.

"He isn't going to shoot anyone. Once he gets inside, my natural charm will go to work."

Laura snickered.

"But, if he starts to leave, you have to move in and stop him. Don't hurt him—just stop him."

"You'd better hope he doesn't hurt *you*," Laura said sarcastically.

Charlie and Laura bought two sodas from the machine while Kerry and Pete retreated to chairs by the potato sacks. The large wall clock showed 7:15.

Charlie began arranging his checkers. "I hope he hasn't been here. All you have to do is relax," he explained. "When Captain Rankin comes through that door, I'll have my eye on him. If we look cool, he'll know we have things under control. That's it, guys—just relax. It's your move, Laura."

Laura took a drink of soda and moved a checker.

Charlie pushed his checker while keeping one eye on the door.

"You're doing great, lady. You look relaxed."

Laura took another drink.

BANG!

The sound startled Laura, and she spit her soda all over Charlie. Just as the spray hit his chest, Charlie dropped back in his chair and fell to the floor.

"Got him!" Woody exclaimed. "Finally got that pesky fly." He held up his green fly swatter.

"A fly swatter?" Charlie asked, as he climbed to his feet.

"Mr. Cool," Laura jeered. "You didn't look so charming falling out of your chair."

"Me? I didn't spit soda all over everybody."

Charlie stood looking at his shirt. The front was splattered with soda as if a shotgun had sprayed buckshot all over him. Everyone was laughing except Charlie.

Charlie sank down into his chair. "You're going to frighten him away by clowning around."

"Who's clowning?"

"Be quiet and move."

"Be quiet and move," Laura mimicked.

"It's a wonder I ever get anything done hanging around you melon-heads. I'm willing to stare danger square in the face, but it's hard when I'm surrounded by turkeys."

"Pity, pity," Laura mocked.

Snap, snap, snap, snap.

"Oh, my!" she intoned. "I accidentally took four of your men."

Whack! Whack!

"Kerry's hand is stuck," Pete announced.

"In what?" Charlie barked.

"A pickle jar," Kerry said meekly.

"A pickle jar?" Laura fumed.

Charlie rubbed his hand over his face. "Any minute, the Captain is going to come crashing through that door. I'm sprayed with soda from Little Miss Fire Hydrant; and the guy who is supposed to help me, has his hand stuck in a pickle jar."

"I didn't mean to."

"Pete," Charlie called, "get a bigger jar and put his head in it."

The clock kept ticking as everyone settled down to wait quietly. It was now 8:15 and no word from the Captain.

"How long are we going to stick around?" Kerry asked.

"I don't know," Charlie answered without moving. He and Laura had long ago stopped playing checkers. "It's too soon to go home. He has to show up."

"What time do you close, Woody?" Laura asked.

"Not till nine," he answered pleasantly.

"Let's face it, Charlie, he isn't coming." Laura crushed her aluminum soda can in her hand.

"We can wait until nine. If he doesn't show, we'll have to go back out to that dumb freighter. I'm in no hurry to do that."

"What do you think that noise was from the other room in the ship?" Laura asked.

"That's no big deal. I figure it has to be a tape recording," Charlie said. "Did you notice the screaming usually started after Captain Rankin went into the room?"

"You're probably right," Laura concluded. "For sure it wasn't that goofy mannequin we rescued."

"How did we know? It had to be rescued."

"You ought to take it down to the newspaper and have your picture taken. I can see the headline now— 'Chesapeake Charlie Leads Daring Rescue Party To Save Rubber Mannequin.' You won't need to mention my name."

"Just drop it."

"The sub-headline will read, 'Mannequin had been held for months without food or water.' "

"Forget it."

"Here, give me your soda can. I'll show you a trick."

Laura took the aluminum can and set it upright on the floor.

"I saw somebody do this on television."

Carefully balancing herself, Laura stood on the can with one foot. The can held its form as she moved her arms to stop from tilting.

Steadying herself, Laura reached down and gently tapped the can on both sides. It crushed immediately into a heap.

"Please, please, don't applaude—just throw money."

Pete walked over to Charlie. "This is boring. Let's forget it and go home."

Kerry rubbed his sore wrist. "Yeah, it's almost nine now."

"Well, Charlie, there went another great plan down the drain," Laura said as she stepped toward the door. "Back to the old drawing board."

"This is worse than you think." Charlie sounded somber. "We've taken Captain Rankin's silver candleholders and left him with practically nothing. He's liable to do something desperate. Now we really do need a good plan."

"So what do we do now?" Kerry asked.

"I know it's late, but we have to try it. The only thing to do is grab a boat and go back out to the ship. Maybe we can talk the Captain into coming ashore."

"And how do we do that?" Laura sounded exasperated. "Don't tell me—'your natural charm.'"

"You've got it. Let's run."

They hurried outside and clattered down the wooden steps while Woody closed his store. Dodging trees, they darted through the forest in the direction of Charlie's house.

"Let's take the green boat," Pete suggested.

"Kerry, you row," Charlie directed.

"Why me?"

They dragged the boat over to the water and pushed it out from the shore.

"Hey!" Pete yelled.

"What in the world?" Laura puzzled.

"Look what's happened," Kerry said. "The bottom of the boat has been chopped out. It's just sinking."

"What low-life would do that?" He looked around, not really expecting to see anyone.

"Listen," whispered Pete, lifting his drowned foot from the boat. "There's a noise."

"It's only a twig," Kerry insisted.

Laura tried to see through the darkness. "I'm not so sure."

Charlie said, "Shhh. There it is again." He squinted his eyes. "Who is it?" he called in a loud whisper.

"You guys are imagining things," Kerry said.

Charlie called out, "Whoever you are, come over here by the pier." He moved away from the boat.

Whunk! A stone hit the boat causing all four of them to jerk with fear.

"It *is* somebody," Laura whispered, and reached down to pick up a stick.

Charlie reached for a broken board.

"Hee, Hee, Hee!" came the reply.

Chapter Ten

"Fan out, but be careful," Charlie whispered, motioning with his hands. He raised his voice. "We're glad to hear you, Captain Rankin. We were going out to see you."

"Hee, Hee, Hee!" came back slowly with a spooky roll to it.

"We have your candlesticks," Laura said, and moved to her left. "We only took them so we could help you—honest!"

"Be careful," Pete whispered. "He has that musket."

Charlie stood still. "I'm sure we can help you, Captain Rankin. Why don't you come closer so we can talk? Come on, we're friends."

"Hee, Hee, Hee!"

Pete broke from the group and raced to the left between the trees.

Thump! "Ahhhhh!"

Charlie looked over to see Pete sprawled flat on his face.

"Hee, Hee, Hee!"

Laura felt goose pimples stand up on her arm.

Kerry said unsteadily, "Captain Rankin, let's make a deal. We'll be happy to return your candleholders. Come over here and let's talk about it."

"On four—" Charlie whispered, "on four we all run."

"He has a gun," Laura hissed.

"He probably can't hit a moving target—and it's dark. We'll meet at Anderson's backyard. On four."

"Hee, Hee, Hee!"

"One. Two. Three. Four."

They dashed in all directions: Charlie around the house, Laura along the shoreline, and Pete behind the boats.

Only Kerry failed to make a clean getaway. He tumbled and fell flat on his stomach.

"Hee, Hee, Hee!"

Captain Rankin wrestled Kerry's arm against his back in a painful position.

"If you fight, it will only hurt more."

Roughly he tied Kerry's hands behind him.

Laura was the first to arrive breathlessly at Andersons. Charlie and Pete soon followed. Pete held his side because of the throbbing pain.

"Where's Kerry?" Laura asked.

"I didn't see him," Charlie gasped, resting his hands on his knees to help his breathing. "Maybe he went the long way around."

Several minutes passed while they regained their strength. There was still no sign of Kerry.

"I hope Rankin didn't get him," Laura said fearfully.

Charlie leaned against a tree. "We'll have to go back and check."

"Why don't we just call the police?" Pete asked. "He could really get hurt."

"There isn't time. We have to go right back." Charlie led the way in a steady trot.

"Kerry! Kerry!" Pete called.

"Don't lose your cool," Charlie said. "We'll find him. Spread out, but don't lose sight of each other."

"Hee, Hee, Hee!"

Pete froze, motionless as a statue.

Charlie yelled with a shaky voice, "Where's Kerry?"

"Hee, Hee, Hee!" was all the answer that came. The hair on the back of Charlie's neck stiffened.

"Where's Laura?" Charlie whispered.

Pete stepped closer to Charlie. "She was right here."

"Captain Rankin, you can't get away with this." Charlie called. "Our parents will be home any minute. What do you want?"

"My candleholders. Hee, Hee, Hee!"

"It's a deal," Pete said. "We'll never mess with your stuff again. Charlie, go get those candlesticks."

"Fair enough," Charlie agreed. "I can show you exactly where they are, Captain."

Suddenly, Pete broke for a clearing. Charlie hesitated for a minute, and then rushed in the opposite direction.

As Pete cut around the garage, something grabbed him.

Captain Rankin stuffed a cloth in his mouth. Stumbling and swaying, Pete fell to the ground. Captain Rankin sat on top of Pete and tied the cloth around his mouth, silencing him. He then twisted his arms behind him and tied them tightly.

Pete was led behind the boats where Kerry and Laura were bound. Pete's hands were tied to a rope that held the other two. None of them could budge or make a sound.

"Three down and one to go, Hee, Hee, Hee!"

Charlie realized he was alone. He had underestimated the ability of the crafty sailor. Maybe he had gotten his friends into serious trouble. Cautiously, Charlie inched back.

A plan, a plan, Charlie thought. Charlie's mind raced for a solution, some means of attack.

An idea began to take form. Carefully, he backed up and climbed onto the toolshed roof.

Nothing moved. There was no breeze to disturb the night air. Not a shadow shifted, not a twig twisted. The backyard was still and silent.

Charlie's own breathing sounded like a hurricane roaring through his head. He tried to breathe softly, in shorter motions.

Snap! Snap! Charlie arched his arms back and lunged off the shed. He pounced on his victim. "Got you!" Charlie screamed as he landed.

"Arf! Arf!" Cries shattered the silence as Charlie wrestled his enemy across the ground. "Arf Arf!" A bewildered beagle fought to free itself from the strange creature from outer space.

"Throckmorton! Oh, no." Charlie let go of his dog.

"Hee, Hee, Hee! Hands on your head, my little friend." Captain Rankin held his musket barrel tightly against Charlie's back. "Do anything foolish and you'll be crab bait. Now, put your left hand behind your back—slowly."

Charlie twisted his left hand slowly behind him. Suddenly, his right hand shot toward Captain Rankin, knocking the musket from his grasp. Charlie turned and dove for the Captain's ankles. Rankin's feet scrambled in opposite directions. The Captain stumbled backwards and fell like an old tree.

The two began to wrestle fiercely on the dew-soaked ground. Charlie managed a headlock on the Captain, but his victim merely tossed him over his shoulder. Captain Rankin stood up and ran for his musket.

Frantically, Charlie jumped to his feet and lunged for the Captain's back. He leaped up on him in piggyback fashion.

"Let go, you snake-eyed sea serpent!"

Captain Rankin fought hard to throw off his young rider. Like a rodeo bull, he bucked and kicked, but Charlie held tightly to his back.

The double-decked pair staggered wildly around the yard. The Captain yelled a long list of threats. At a pile of old boards, Rankin lost his footing and they both went tumbling over the heap.

"What is going on?" a voice called gruffly.

Charlie had never been so glad to hear his father's voice. Mr. Dean stood over the tangle of legs and arms. He held Captain Rankin's musket in his hand.

"The garage is really looking great," Laura teased as she stared up at Charlie.

Charlie stood on a six foot ladder and took wide swipes with his paint brush.

"Looks like you're grounded and having to paint the garage."

"Pete acted like the whole thing was *my* idea—the creep!" Charlie spread another ribbon of white paint. "He didn't even go with me to tell the police about the man in the tan hat."

"They didn't have any trouble catching him," Laura said. "He was the only person around St. Michaels wearing a tan hat."

Charlie took two more broad strokes with his

brush. "They say he'll be behind bars for a long time."

"I don't see how they can ever straighten out the candlestick mess," Laura said.

"You didn't see this morning's paper," Charlie said, dipping his brush in the bucket. "They couldn't figure out a fair way to settle up, so the jewelry store agreed to pay Captain Rankin a large amount of money. They said that they felt sorry for the man—and besides, they had bought the holders very cheaply."

"Well, then it's working out a lot better than I thought it would," Laura said.

"Sure, easy for you to say. I'm stuck up on this ladder."

"They said that if no one pressed charges, Captain Rankin should be able to go home soon."

"Sure, and I'm stuck up on this ladder."

"Is that all you do—complain?"

"Complain? I'm the only one who got punished. I have to paint this crummy garage. Then I have to hang around the house for three weeks. Boy, were my parents mad."

"Well, it kind of was your idea. You knew your parents told you not to do it."

"I think you'd better leave," he grunted.

"I think I will. I have lots to do. After all, *I'm* not grounded."

"You ought to be. You ought to be grounded just for being weird."

"All I know is that I could have gotten shot, just because you insisted on doing what your parents told you not to do. Now, who's weird?"

"Buzz off, vulture breath."

"You know what your problem is? I'll tell you. You have chicken liver for brains."

"I warned you, crab face."

Charlie held the paint brush in his right hand and ran his left hand firmly across the stiff bristles. Paint sprayed into the air and shot across Laura's face, leaving a hundred white freckles.

"You, you, you. . . . ." Laura grabbed the open bucket of white paint from the ladder.

"Now, quit that, Laura. You're getting carried away. I'll tell your parents, Laura."

She threw the paint up toward Charlie, splashing it across the front of his pants. Quickly she tossed it again, this time sending the bucket along.

"That's it! That's it!" Charlie yelled, sliding down the paint-soaked steps. "You've had it."

Laura ran around the house and rushed down the paved highway.

Charlie followed twenty yards behind, waving his wet brush in the air. "Come back!" he yelled. "Come back!"